NANNY FOR THE DON

AN AGE GAP, BILLIONAIRE ROMANCE

K.C. CROWNE

When's the worst time to meet your insanely hot, older boss?
Probably when he's naked in the shower…
Doing something obscene… and equally fascinating.

Taking the job as Nico Conti's nanny seemed perfect.
Just me, two sweet girls, and a payday before Christmas.
But my first day was a total disaster.
By nightfall, I'm soaking in his luxurious tub, thinking he's out of town.
But then I hear footsteps—my heart leaps into my throat as I slide deeper into the bubbles.
Nico steps into the shower, every inch of him gloriously on display.
And what I see him doing… I *definitely* shouldn't be watching.

Day two: he catches me in the library, wearing a flimsy robe, reading something I shouldn't.
The way his eyes darken sends a thrill through me.

Day three: I nearly set his immaculate kitchen on fire.
And that's when things *really* start to heat up.

Nico isn't just your average billionaire.
He's a ruthless Don.

And when he finds out I'm carrying his child, he doesn't leave any room for interpretation: I'm his now. No choice. No turning back. No escape.

Readers note: This is full-length standalone, Christmas, single dad, billionaire's nanny, mafia, age-gap, romance. No cheating. HEA guaranteed.

CHAPTER 1

WILLOW

I'm naked in my billionaire boss's tub, about five seconds away from losing my job.

Not exactly how I pictured my first day ending.

I sink deeper into the warm water, letting lavender-scented bubbles rise to my chin, trying to convince myself that I'm not out of my goddamn mind.

Honestly, it's like I completely forgot who *owns* this place. Mr. Conti's twins wore me down to the bone, and somewhere between bath time and bedtime, logic made a run for it, leaving me here in his absurdly luxurious bathroom like I have a right to it.

A soft smile tugs at my lips as I remember the girls' antics from earlier. They're trouble, but the cute kind, with wide eyes and endless energy. It's only day one, and they've already wormed their way into my heart. I already feel like I'd do just about anything for them.

That is, of course, assuming I don't get fired for turning my boss's sacred tub into my own personal spa day.

I close my eyes, letting exhaustion wrap around me like a warm blanket.

Just a few minutes, I think.

Just to pretend I belong here, soaking in marble-covered, bubbly bliss like a pampered rich kid. *Just me, and the glorious silence.*

But then... I hear it.

Footsteps. Heavy, unmistakable, and—oh, hell—coming closer.

My eyes fly open, and panic bolts through me like a shot of espresso.

No, no, no.

He's supposed to be gone.

Out of town.

Off doing whatever intimidating billionaires do. But those footsteps are real, closing in, echoing through his private sanctuary, and I'm naked as the day I was born.

Move, Willow. *Move!*

But my body's frozen, clinging to the last shred of hope that maybe he's just walking by, maybe he won't actually come in here.

Please, universe, help me out here.

And then, miraculously, he doesn't storm in to throw me out or fire me on the spot. No, Mr. Conti—the man whose pristine bathroom I'm currently defiling—heads straight for the shower instead.

I release a shaky breath, clinging to the tiny scrap of sanity I have left.

I know I should get out now, quietly sneak back to the guest room, and act like none of this ever happened. But then I hear the water start, and just like that, curiosity kicks in, silencing the voice of reason in my head.

Just one little peek...

After all, I've already seriously crossed the line—what's one more tiny step?

I slide my gaze through the smallest crack in the curtain—and nearly forget how to breathe.

Holy shit.

Nico Conti stands under the spray, water cascading down his sculpted back, tracing every ridge and dip of muscle. His shoulders are broad, his stance powerful. The man looks like he was crafted out of stone, every inch of him honed to perfection. Like something out of my deepest, most shameful fantasies—a walking, dripping masterpiece of a man who probably doesn't even realize he's this unfairly hot.

The way the water runs down his sculpted back, tracing every hard line of muscle, all the way down to that perfect, firm ass.

Damn.

Seriously, the man could be a walking advertisement for whatever workout routine he's punishing himself with. Water streams down his skin, gleaming over each sculpted muscle. His hair, flecked with the perfect amount of distinguished gray, screams *'silver fox alert,'* adding an air of seasoned charisma that makes him even more irresistible.

I'm not even into older men... well, I wasn't. But now? One look at Nico, and something inside me is switching on that I didn't even know was there.

I watch him soap up, his hands gliding over every contour of those rock-hard muscles. I'm practically drooling as I trace the path his fingers take, lathering up every inch of his body. And just when I think I might be able to tear myself away, he reaches for the soap, running his hands over his chest, down his torso, and—oh God—right over his cock.

His glorious cock.

I clap a hand over my mouth to hold back a gasp. My pulse quickens, my breath catching in my throat as I watch him, totally mesmerized. His hand moves over his cock. And it's not just any cock—it's thick, and it's hard.

Oh, sweet hell.

It's far more stunning than I ever could've imagined, and suddenly my mind goes straight to the gutter, every single thought sinful. I've never actually seen one in person before, let alone one that... looks like that. All I can think about is him, the feel of his body, his hands running down my skin, his hips pressing against mine, stretching me in ways I've only dared to dream.

I shake my head, trying to push those thoughts away.

Focus, Willow! You've got to get out of here without getting caught.

Here I am at 23, a virgin, standing stupidly behind a curtain, spying on my older, undeniably hot boss.

This is fine. Everything's fine.

My heart races, and I'm torn between running away and watching just a moment longer. Just when I think it couldn't get any worse, he lets out a low, guttural moan that makes my stomach flip. Then he says something that nearly knocks me out of the tub.

"Take it all, Willow," he groans, voice dark and rough.

Wait, what?! I'm stunned, heart racing so fast I feel dizzy. *Take it all?* My brain barely processes that he's... he's thinking of me. I'm the reason he's touching himself in the shower. That's the only way he'd know my name... he's been watching my yoga videos on YouTube, watching me in my leggings, all those poses, and...

Holy shit.

Flattered doesn't even begin to cover it. The idea of this insanely hot older man getting off to me is enough to make my head spin. I can't look away, my gaze glued to the way his muscles ripple with every movement, the way his hand works up and down his cock in an unhurried, steady rhythm. He's completely lost in his pleasure, and part of me aches to be the one making him feel that way. The thought sends a thrill through me, a spark that leaves me warm and breathless.

I catch sight of the detachable shower head, and before I can second-guess it, I reach for it, my hand trembling as I bring the water down between my legs. The first pulse of water against my clit makes me gasp, a wave of pleasure crashing over me. I close my eyes, drowning in the fantasy.

In my mind, I'm there with him, pressed against his hard, wet body, my hands exploring every inch, every ripple of muscle. I imagine him turning, that smoldering, intense gaze locking onto mine, the heat between us flaring as his hands slide down my back, pulling me against him. He lifts me, my legs wrapping around his waist as he presses me against the wall, his cock filling me with every rough thrust.

The fantasy is so real I can barely think straight, my body heating up with every pulsing sensation. His voice echoes in my mind, low and commanding. "You like this, don't you?" he growls, his breath hot against my ear. "You like the way I'm fucking you, don't you, Willow?"

"Yes... yes," I gasp, clinging to him in my mind, my body writhing under the pulse of the water. *God, yes.* Every imagined thrust sends a shiver down my spine, and I'm teetering on the edge, feeling every pulse, every beat of desire echo through me.

And then, in the real world, I hear it—he moans my name, rough and desperate—and that's it. My entire body clenches, pleasure crashing over me in waves as I come, hard, biting my lip to keep from crying out. I imagine him there with me, filling me, the heat between us leaving us both breathless and spent.

As the intensity fades, I take a steadying breath, my body still tingling from the aftershocks. I peek through the curtain again, just to be sure. Nico's braced against the wall, his chest heaving as he takes in deep, steady breaths.

It's my cue. Time to get out before I do something even more insane. I grab the towel, wrap it around myself, and slip out of the tub as quietly as possible, my heart racing the entire time. Each step feels like a high-stakes escape, but finally, I'm out of the bathroom, and relief washes over me.

Back in the bedroom, I let out a shaky laugh, my entire body still buzzing from the close call. But as I turn to leave, something catches my eye—and it stops me dead in my tracks.

His suit. Laid out neatly on the bed, like it's waiting for him. That faint, warm, spicy scent wraps around me, and my knees threaten to give out.

I can't help myself; I lean in, inhaling the scent that's unmistakably him, feeling a fresh thrill race down my spine.

Focus, Willow, I tell myself, forcing my feet to keep moving. I'm halfway to the door, ready to make a clean escape when it hits me.

I left the baby monitor in the bathroom.

My eyes widen, dread flooding my veins.

Shit.

Ms. M warned me that the girls sometimes wake up and wander around at night. And if they do, they'll be on their own—completely unsupervised.

A shiver runs through me as the realization sinks in: there's no choice.

I have to go back. I have to slip past him, through the steam-filled bathroom where he's still in the shower, and retrieve that damn monitor.

CHAPTER 2

NICO

A blast of cold water shocks me back to my senses, a harsh contrast to the heat that had me unwinding just a minute ago.

I shut off the water and reach for a towel, jaw clenched, mind replaying the scene that just unfolded in my head. The slight shift in the bath curtains, the closed door, the faint scent of lavender that wasn't mine—small details that add up now, with Willow's face fresh in my mind.

How the hell did I miss that someone had been in here? The last time I'd been that distracted was... never. It was a rookie mistake, and I don't make rookie mistakes. Yet here I am, towel around my waist, glaring at the shower curtain as if it has answers.

I wrap the towel tighter and stride back into the bedroom, forcing myself to shake off the irritation. The snow falls gently outside my window, a deceptive calm settling over the city. But tonight is anything but calm. There's work to be done, and I'll be extracting answers from the men who think silence can shield them. It'll be the kind of night that calls for focus, clarity, and not an ounce of distraction.

Just as I'm getting my head back in the game, a knock at my door pulls me out of it. I pause, irritation flaring, but a sliver of curiosity edges in, too. I walk over, grip the handle, and open it, and there she is—the woman I'd just pictured in ways I shouldn't be thinking about my employees.

"Hi." Her voice is soft, almost unsure, and there's a slight shiver to her, like she'd been gathering up the courage just to knock.

She's wearing nothing but a loose sleep shirt and a pair of shorts that hug her legs, long and toned in a way I hadn't fully appreciated until now. In the dim hallway light, she's beautiful, almost ethereal, like a strange dream I hadn't planned on walking right into. And she's not wearing a bra, which makes the situation more awkward—and yet, I can't look away.

"Hi," I respond, leaning casually against the door frame, trying not to let on how my mind is replaying the scene from the shower in the harshest detail.

She clears her throat. "I'm Willow, the new nanny." Her eyes dart over my chest, lingering on the tattoos, the scars, like she's studying something unexpected.

"I know who you are," I say, my voice a bit harder than I intend. Her shoulders stiffen, and I catch the flicker of nerves in her expression.

"I'm sorry to bother you," she begins, already shifting on her feet.

"What do you need, Willow?" I don't mean for my tone to sound so direct, but the edge is there, part irritation, part curiosity. I want to know exactly why she's standing here, fresh out of the memory of my shower, looking at me like this.

She takes a deep breath. "I... I took a bath in your tub earlier," she admits, her voice barely a whisper. "And I left the iPad for the baby monitor in your bathroom. I know the girls sometimes wander at night, and I didn't want to risk them being unsupervised... even if it meant coming here."

Her cheeks turn pink, and she quickly adds, "If I've overstepped, I completely understand, and I'll pack my things and leave first thing in the morning."

She stands there, a nervous tension visible in every line of her face, clearly bracing herself for a reprimand. And she's right—she did cross a line. But she's here, owning up to it, something I don't often see in people who work for me. And hell, she's not just any nanny, clearly.

"Wait here," I say, turning on my heel to head back to the bathroom. I yank back the curtain and there it is, resting on the tub's edge just like she said. I pick up the iPad, press the screen, and the baby monitor app lights up, showing my daughters' peaceful, sleeping faces. Relief eases the last bit of tension in my chest, but there's an edge of irritation, too—how had I missed this?

I had been so... distracted that I didn't notice. That was a mistake, and I don't let my guard down. Not ever. Pushing down the annoyance, I stride back out to find Willow waiting, her shoulders stiff, her eyes wide with anticipation.

I hold out the iPad to her. "Here," I say, watching as she reaches out, almost hesitant.

Her fingers curl around it, and I can see her relief, though she tries to mask it. "I'm really sorry," she says, stumbling over her words. "I was exhausted, and my bathroom only has a shower, and I thought..." She stops herself, realizing she's rambling. It's strangely endearing.

I can't help the smirk that forms, though I school it quickly. She catches the expression and visibly tenses, expecting the worst, as if I'm about to explode and fire her on the spot.

"Relax," I say, holding up a hand. "I'm not going to fire you." I let out a breath. "Olivia gave you high marks for today, and I'm not in the habit of letting go of good nannies for a simple mistake."

She looks like she might collapse in relief, and it's almost amusing, the way her entire posture relaxes as she takes a shaky breath. I lean against the door frame, crossing my arms, and I don't miss the way her eyes flick to my arms and chest.

"You know," I continue, enjoying the flush on her cheeks, "I'm a little impressed. Not only did you have the guts to sneak into your boss's bathroom, but you were willing to own up to it because you wanted to make sure you did your job right."

She blushes deeper, her innocence and nerves both ridiculously appealing. I don't miss how her gaze shifts, her lips parting slightly. It's both a bit naive and a bit bold, and hell, I can't remember the last time I felt this drawn to someone so different from my world.

"You're serious?" she asks, voice barely above a whisper.

"Yes. But there's one condition." I hold up a finger.

She nods, eager. "Anything."

"Total honesty from here on out," I say, meeting her gaze directly. "In my world, trust is rare, and I'd like to keep things straight between us. My daughters... they tend to stretch the truth when they're in trouble. If I can at least count on you to be upfront, that's one less thing to worry about."

Relief, mixed with determination, flashes in her eyes. "Absolutely. Nothing but the truth from here on out."

"Good." I give her a nod. "Then we'll be fine."

Her face lights up in a small, shy smile. "Thank you. Really. Not just for letting this slide, but for giving me a chance with your girls. They're amazing, and I'm going to make sure you don't regret hiring me."

"See that you don't."

We stand there for a moment, and there's a charged energy lingering between us, the memory of earlier still fresh in my mind. Her eyes drop slightly, as though she's only just realized how close we're standing.

"I'm sorry again about the tub. And... it was nice to officially meet you." She gives me a small, tentative smile. "Good night, Mr. Conti."

Before she turns away, I reach out, my hand finding her arm, a gentle but intentional touch that stops her. Her breath catches, and I can feel the tension, the ripple of awareness between us as her gaze locks onto mine.

"You're welcome to use the tub," I tell her, my voice dropping just enough to let her know I mean it. "When I'm not home. Which is often."

She nods, her eyes lighting up. "Thank you. That's... really generous of you."

"Good night, Willow," I say, letting my hand drop.

She nods, turning to leave, and this time, I let my gaze follow her down the hall, watching the subtle sway of her hips as she disappears into the darkness.

CHAPTER 3

WILLOW

I wake up to the morning light streaming into my room, a big, goofy smile plastered across my face as the realization hits—I still have a freaking job.

I half-expected to find my things packed up with a polite-but-firm note asking me to leave after last night's close call, but nope, here I am. Willow, officially still employed. I check my phone and blink in surprise; I'm up a full thirty minutes before my alarm. *Score.*

With a little extra time to spare before I need to get the twins up, my mind—traitor that it is—drifts immediately to Mr. Conti. Nico. Shirtless. Gray sweatpants hanging low, sculpted chest still damp. I practically shiver, remembering how absurdly good he looked, the image permanently seared into my brain. And did he realize how perfectly those sweatpants outlined his... assets?

A thrill shoots through me, and just like that, I'm turned on. *Again.*

Biting my lip, I slide my hand down, slipping it underneath my panties. My fingers find their way to my clit, and I close my eyes, letting the memory of Nico flood my mind—shirtless, powerful, with that intense gaze that made me feel completely bare. In my fantasy, I'm back in his room, caught in the act. Except this time, he notices.

He catches me staring at him, a wicked smirk lifting the corner of his mouth.

"Like what you see?" His voice is low, teasing.

I nod, barely able to find my voice. "Yes," I whisper, my throat dry.

In one swift movement, he's in front of me, closing the distance between us in an instant. His hands grip my waist, pulling me against him, his body radiating heat, his thick cock pressing hard against my stomach. Before I can react, his mouth is on mine, kissing me with a hunger that leaves me breathless. I clutch his shoulders, melting into him, helpless against the force of his desire.

He pulls back just enough to whisper, "You know I have to punish you for last night, don't you?"

A thrill shoots through me as I meet his smoldering gaze. "What kind of punishment?"

He doesn't answer. Instead, he takes my hand and leads me back to the bed, shutting the door behind us with a decisive click. His eyes are dark, intense, and I know I'm in for it.

"Get on your knees," he commands, his voice a low growl.

I sink to the floor without question, heart pounding as I watch him grip the waistband of those sweatpants. He tugs them down, and there it is—thick, hard, everything I've been craving. My mouth waters, and I look up at him, waiting, needing his approval.

"Go on," he murmurs, nodding. "Show me how much you want it."

I lean forward, my lips wrapping around him, savoring the salty, masculine taste as I start to move, slow and deliberate. His hands thread through my hair, gripping tight as he watches me, his jaw tight, eyes dark and hooded. He looks like a god, standing over me, his body tense with control, every inch of him radiating power.

In reality, my breath catches as the climax builds, my fingers moving frantically to finish myself off. And when it hits, I have to bite my lip to keep from crying out, the pleasure crashing over me like a wave. My body trembles as I ride it out, panting, hand clamped over my mouth, trying not to moan too loudly.

Finally, I lie there, completely spent, feeling a mix of bliss and shock. *That man is dangerous,* I think, a thrill shooting through me at just how real he feels in my fantasies.

But I'm snapped back to reality by my alarm, its shrill ring jolting me out of bed. I roll out, get dressed, and make my way down the hall to the twins' room, still buzzing from the morning's private... activity.

As I open the door, a smile tugs at my lips. The girls' room is straight out of a fairy tale, all pink walls with tiny white stars, a cloud-shaped rug, and shelves overflowing with stuffed animals that look like they're in a perpetual tea party. And there they are—Giulia and Lucia, snuggled up in their little beds, completely oblivious to the chaos of yesterday.

They look so peaceful, their faces soft and angelic, curls spilling over their pillows. For a second, I almost feel bad waking them. But I've got a job to do, and it's time to get these little whirlwinds up and ready for the day.

I walk over to Giulia's bed, gently brushing her shoulder. "Good morning, sunshine," I whisper, trying to sound as cheerful as I can. She stirs, mumbling something incoherent as she burrows deeper into her blankets.

I remember Ms. M's little trick for telling them apart— Giulia has a tiny smattering of freckles behind her left ear. Sure enough, there they are, my tiny lifeline in the world of identical twins.

"Giulia," I whisper softly.

She opens her eyes, blinking up at me with those big, dark eyes that remind me so much of her dad. There's a striking resemblance, the same intense gaze even when she's barely awake.

"Morning, sleepyhead," I say, smiling as she rubs her eyes.

"Hi," she mumbles, her voice all sleepy and soft.

"Hi yourself," I grin, giving her a gentle pat. "Time to get up, kiddo. We've got a big day ahead!"

Giulia nods sleepily, and I move over to Lucia, who's still fast asleep. I try the same gentle shake on her shoulder, but she just pulls the blanket over her head with a grumpy little grumble.

"Come on, Lucia! Rise and shine! The day's not gonna start itself!" I tease, tugging the blanket down just enough to see her pouty face.

"Nooo," she whines, clinging to the last remnants of sleep.

"Oh yes," I say, chuckling as I pull the blanket off her. "Time to wake up, princess. We've got all sorts of fun planned today!"

Lucia lets out an exaggerated sigh, finally giving in as she stretches her little arms. "Fine," she says, her tone overly dramatic, and I can't help but laugh.

We start with brushing our teeth, and I make up a silly song about sparkly teeth and chasing away sugar bugs, which has them in giggles as they try to sing along.

"Brush, brush, brush those pearly whites!" I chant, dancing around like a goofball. "Make the sugar bugs run for their lives!"

By the time we're done, their teeth are gleaming, and they're in fits of laughter. We move on to getting dressed, and I go over the basics of bed-making with them—Ms. M said they were just learning, so we make a little game out of it.

"See? Just like this," I say, demonstrating as they eagerly try to copy me. The results are... well, let's just say "neat" is a work in progress. But the proud look on their faces is worth every lopsided blanket and slightly flattened pillow.

With the beds passably made, I turn to them with a grin. "Now, who's ready for breakfast?"

"Me!" they both shout, practically bouncing.

"Alright, what do you feel like?"

"Pizza!" Giulia says confidently.

"And ice cream!" Lucia chimes in like it's the most obvious breakfast choice ever.

I shake my head, laughing. "Nice try. How about pancakes instead?"

Their eyes light up. "Pancakes!" they cheer, and we head to the kitchen.

As we make our way downstairs, I can't help but glance around, relieved to find no sign of Mr. Conti. It's probably better for my heart rate if he's nowhere in sight this morning.

On the way down, I ask, "So, does your dad ever decorate for Christmas?"

Lucia shrugs. "We don't know."

"Can we get a Christmas tree?" Giulia asks, her eyes sparkling.

"Absolutely we're getting a tree!" I declare, already imagining this place decked out in holiday cheer. Whether Mr. Conti likes it or not, these girls are getting Christmas magic.

In the kitchen, I pause for a moment, taking in the morning light streaming through the big windows and the dusting of snow outside. "Alright, pancakes coming up!" I say, rubbing my hands together. I spot a fancy espresso machine on the counter and feel a pang of longing. "Too bad I have no idea how to use this thing..."

Giulia's eyes light up. "I know how!"

I blink, surprised. "You do?"

"Uh-huh! I watch Daddy all the time," she says confidently.

Before I know it, she's guiding me through the steps, standing on her tiptoes as she instructs me to load the coffee, tamp it down, and press the button. Sure enough, the espresso pours out perfectly, and I'm seriously impressed.

"Wow, little miss barista!" I say, ruffling her hair. "You're a coffee pro."

"Daddy says coffee is 'really, really important,'" she says, giggling.

With espresso in hand and the girls laughing, I feel ready to tackle the day. We grab ingredients for the pancakes, and I enlist the twins' help, which quickly turns into a kitchen circus. Giulia tries to crack an egg, but it ends up all over the counter.

Lucia spills milk, and somehow, flour explodes into a cloud, coating us all in a fine layer of powder. I try to laugh it off, but honestly, I'm questioning my decision to make pancakes with two enthusiastic little sous-chefs.

"Okay, no worries!" I say, keeping my voice upbeat as I swipe flour off my forehead. "This is just... extra fun!"

The girls giggle, their faces dusted white, looking like tiny bakers in training. We finally manage to get a decent batter mixed, and I pour the first dollop into the pan. But as I turn back to check on them, I catch a whiff of something burning. My heart skips as I realize I've left a dish towel too close to the burner.

I snatch it up, toss it into the sink, and douse it with water just as the smoke alarm starts blaring. The twins shriek, covering their ears, and I fan the air frantically, praying this isn't going to wake up the whole household.

As if on cue, Ms. M walks into the kitchen, her eyes widening as she takes in the chaos—the flour-covered counter, sugar everywhere, pancake batter splattered on the cabinets, and me, looking like I've survived a food fight.

"What on earth is going on here?" she asks, hands on her hips but with a smile tugging at her lips.

I stand there, caught red-handed, flour and milk all over me. "Uh... pancakes?"

"We'll discuss this later."

Those had been Ms. M's words after seeing the destruction in the kitchen. After making sure the fire was out and confirming the girls and the house were safe, she'd left it at that.

Now I'm sitting in the den, trying to shake off the nerves while the twins enjoy their allotted hour of TV time before dinner. They're watching *Bluey*, totally engrossed in the antics of the Heeler family, while I'm over here trying not to freak out about the conversation I know is coming.

Thank God Mr. Conti has staff to handle lunch and dinner, so I don't have to deal with the kitchen disaster zone any more than necessary. Tomorrow, I'm sticking to cereal and OJ—no fires, no explosions, just good ol' breakfast simplicity.

Speaking of Mr. Conti, he hasn't shown up at all since this morning. I can't help but wonder how much time he actually gets to spend with his girls, considering his crazy work schedule. I mean, what's the point of having this gorgeous house and adorable kids if you're never around to enjoy them?

Just as I'm lost in thought, Ms. M enters the room, her expression unreadable. "Dinner's ready," she announces, her tone neutral.

I gulp, feeling the anxiety creep back in. I plaster on a smile and get up, mentally preparing myself for whatever Ms. M has in store.

"Alright, ladies, it's chow time!" I say, flicking off the TV. The girls give me matching pouty faces, clearly bummed that *Bluey* time is over, but they're quick to bounce back at the mention of food.

We head to the kitchen instead of the massive, fancy dining room that looks like it's straight out of a magazine but never seems to get used. The girls plop down at the little table, legs swinging as they settle in.

The private chef, a tall woman in her late thirties with sleek black hair pulled into a tight ponytail and an air of effortless elegance, greets us with a warm smile.

"Tonight, we have lemon herb chicken with a side of three-cheese mac and cheese, and roasted asparagus," she announces, her voice smooth and professional. She moves around the kitchen with the grace of someone who's done this a million times.

Giulia tilts her head up at the chef, her big eyes full of hope. "Can we have nuggets instead?" she asks in the sweetest, most innocent voice.

The chef chuckles softly but shakes her head. "Not tonight, sweetie. Maybe another time."

The girls sigh, but they don't protest too much. As we all start to eat, I can feel Ms. M's gaze on me, still not thrilled about the earlier kitchen chaos.

Thankfully, the girls immediately dive into conversation, their little voices full of excitement.

"Ms. M!" Giulia chirps, her fork waving in the air as she talks. "Did you know we saw a squirrel today? It was soooo fluffy!"

Lucia jumps in, not to be outdone. "And it had a big, bushy tail! It was bigger than my arm!"

Ms. M, still holding onto her stern look, softens a bit. "Oh really? And what was this squirrel doing?"

"It was eating a nut!" Giulia says, her eyes wide with the drama of it all. "And then it ran up the tree so fast, like zoom!" She makes a zooming motion with her hand, nearly knocking over her water glass.

Ms. M catches the glass just in time. "That does sound exciting."

Lucia nods eagerly. "And then we tried to find more squirrels, but they were all hiding. Do you think they were playing hide-and-seek?"

Ms. M's expression softens even more. "Maybe they were. Squirrels can be very sneaky like that. Not to mention, it's winter. Squirrels usually stay hidden during this time of year – you're lucky you saw even one."

The girls giggle, clearly pleased with this idea. "Next time, we'll bring them nuts, so they come out and play with us!" Giulia declares.

By this point, Ms. M is definitely smiling, and I can see the tension from earlier melting away. I can't help but feel relieved as I watch the girls work their magic.

Maybe I'll survive today after all.

When dinner's over, I get the girls to bring their plates to the counter. "Good job, ladies," I say, giving them a thumbs-up. They beam at me, proud of their small but important contribution.

Ms. M steps in. "The staff will handle the rest of the cleanup," she says, her tone professional but not unkind.."

"Got it. Thanks," I say, turning to the girls. "Alright, let's head upstairs and get ready for bed."

The girls scamper off, but just as I'm about to follow, Ms. M stops me with a gentle but firm hand on my shoulder. My blood runs cold, and my mind races.

This is it.

Ms. M gives me a steady look. "The safety of the girls and the house isn't something to take lightly."

I nod, swallowing hard. "I know. I'm really sorry about what happened. I'll do better."

But then she surprises me. "That being said, you did a great job with the girls today. They're happy, and they had a good day. That counts for a lot."

Relief floods through me, and I let out a breath. "Thank you, Ms. M. I really appreciate that."

She gives me a small, approving nod. "Just be aware that Mr. Conti will want to discuss the matter with you."

My stomach twists a little at the thought, but I nod again. "I understand."

I head upstairs to join the girls, feeling a lot better than I did just a few minutes ago.

Getting the girls ready for bed this time is a breeze. They're worn out from the day's excitement, so the whole process goes like clockwork. I help them into their pajamas, get them to brush their teeth, and then settle down with them for a couple of bedtime stories. They're so wiped they're both out cold before I even finish the second book.

With the girls tucked in and the house quiet, I realize it's still pretty early. The night is mine, and I'm already thinking about how to spend it. Grabbing the iPad with the monitor, I step into the hall and, half-jokingly, think about how nice it would be to take another soak in Mr. Conti's massive tub. But then I remember the kitchen fiasco and decide maybe I should keep a lower profile tonight.

I also notice Mr. Conti still isn't back. He's been gone all day. I wonder if this is normal for him, being away from the girls so much. It's kind of sad, actually.

As I wander down the hall, I spot the library, a stunning room with cozy sitting areas and shelves packed with books. It looks like the perfect spot to unwind. I step inside, running my fingers along the spines of the books, when Ms.

M suddenly appears, almost. It's like she's materialized out of thin air.

"You're more than welcome to use the library, Willow," she says, her tone neutral. "Just make sure to put everything back where you found it."

"Thanks, Ms. M," I reply, trying to keep my excitement in check.. She nods and walks off, leaving me to hurry inside and explore my new favorite room.

I instantly fall in love with the place. It's like stepping into a scene from one of those old-school, cozy movies. There are several big, high-backed chairs that look like they were made to curl up in with a good book. Off to the side, there's a kid's reading area with an adult-sized chair and the cutest little couch for the twins, perfectly matching and just their size. It's like something out of a storybook.

The towering windows overlook the garden, the soft glow of the outdoor lights illuminating the snowy landscape. And the fireplace! I find the switch and turn it on, watching as the flames flicker to life, instantly filling the room with a warm, inviting glow. The cozy warmth is exactly what I need after the day I've had.

I wonder if Mr. Conti is a big reader. The collection is impressive, but does he ever have the time to actually sit down and enjoy these? Or is this just another part of his life that he barely gets to experience?

Standing in the library, I can't help it—my mind goes straight to the gutter. I imagine Mr. Conti, with those big, strong hands, pushing me down onto the reading table, spreading my legs wide, and pounding into me so hard the books might fall off the shelves.

My thoughts get even filthier—now I'm riding him in one of these big, overstuffed chairs, grinding down on him as he grabs my waist, guiding me into a rhythm that's downright sinful.

And then, the pièce de resistance: himNext, I imagine him on top of me in front of the fireplace, flames flickering on the walls as he takes me with an intensity that leaves me breathless.

I'm so insanely horny right now, I can barely stand it.

Trashy fantasies for a virgin! I scold myself, trying to shake off the heat burning through me.

I take a deep breath and force myself to focus. I need a damn book to get my mind out of the garbage. Scanning the shelves, I finally grab *The Girl with a Clock for a Heart*. A modern mystery— pPerfect. This should be enough to cool me down.

I sink into one of the plush leather chairs, hoping the dark, twisted plot will drown out the dirty thoughts swirling in my head. But as I open the book and start reading, the heat between my legs lingers, teasing me like a memory I can't shake.

I get lost in the book, letting the words pull me in, the flicker of firelight from the fireplace dancing on the pages, and the steady ticking of the grandfather clock grounding me in this cozy, quiet moment. It's almost enough to forget my dirty thoughts.

I'm so invested in the book that when I hear a voice calling my name, I nearly jump out of my skin.

"Willow?"

My heart races as I look up, and there he is, the man himself, standing in the doorway, arms crossed, leaning against the door frame in that effortlessly casual, yet ridiculously sexy way he did last night. The same pose that made me wish he'd just lose control and take me right there.

Mr. Conti's dressed in slacks and dress shoes, with a crisp white button-up that clings to his chest just right, and those damn sleeves are rolled up, showing off his gorgeous forearms.

I can't help but stare, my mind going straight to the gutter again, imagining those hands on me. I'm getting so horny just looking at him, and I can feel my face heating. Then I glance down and realize, to my absolute horror, that I'm sitting here in nothing but my little sleep shorts and a skimpy tank top. No bra. Again.

My nipples are hard, probably visible through the thin fabric, and I know he's noticed. *Shit.* I try to casually cross my arms over my chest, but it's too late—his eyes have already swept over me, lingering just long enough to make my heart pound even harder..

I spring up like a freaking jack-in-the-box, the book flying out of my lap as my eyes go wide. "Uh, I wasn't quite ready for bed," I stammer, trying to sound casual. "Just wanted to grab a book. I'll take it upstairs to my room."

Mr. Conti raises a hand, cutting off my rambling. "Hold on, Willow."

His voice is calm, but his eyes slowly sweep over me, taking in every inch of my barely there outfit.

My face is hot, and I know I'm blushing like crazy. But more than that, I'm getting so damn turned on by the way he's looking at me, like I'm the only thing in the room worth noticing. My pussy clenches, and I swear I can feel myself soaking through my panties.

"You can stay in the library if you want," he says, his voice smooth and inviting. "But first, tell me about the incident in the kitchen."

Damn.

Of course, he'd bring that up. Just when I thought I might survive this encounter without completely embarrassing myself. My mind races, trying to come up with something, anything that doesn't make me look like a total idiot.

But with him standing there, looking all sexy and intense, it's a miracle I even remember how to speak.

CHAPTER 5

"Willow, tell me what happened in the kitchen, and why. Now."

I watch her squirm, her face flushed with a guilty look that's almost too tempting.

God, those fucking legs. I couldn't stop staring at them the moment I walked in. Long, shapely, and strong—perfect. All I can think about is having them wrapped around me, squeezing tight as I'm on top of her, pounding her so hard she can't even think straight.

The way her eyes would roll back as I drive her over the edge, her body trembling under mine.

She's standing in front of me, looking up at me with those wide, innocent eyes, and it's taking everything in me not to drag her out of that chair and make her fantasies a reality.

But I rein it in, keeping my cool.

"I'm sorry. It was stupid, and it'll never happen again."

I shake my head slowly, keeping my gaze steady on hers. "That's not what I want."

Her eyebrows knit together in confusion, those big, expressive eyes searching mine for answers. "Then what do you want?"

"I want to understand what you were thinking."

"The first day with the girls was fun, but a little chaotic," she admits, her voice softening as she recalls the events.says. "I wanted to give them some structure, you know? I mean, kids that age need it. "

I nod slightly, staying quiet, letting her continue.

"The day started off perfectly," she says, a small smile playing on her lips. "I. I got them up, dressed, teeth brushed, beds made—all of it. They were so proud of themselves, and I was, too. So, I figured having them help with breakfast would be good for them."

I raise an eyebrow, amused at how animated she's becoming as she talks about it.

"But then I realized I might've bitten off more than I could chew. The batter was everywhere, chocolate chips were rolling off the counter, and at one point, Giulia tried to crack an egg—except she missed the bowl entirely. We were all laughing so hard, and honestly, they loved every second of it."

I watch her closely, noticing the way her face lights up when she talks about them. She's already crazy about my girls.

She continues, her voice steady but tinged with a bit of regret. "Then things got a little out of hand... as you heard. The girls made a few messes, then I got distracted, and *bam* – fire in the kitchen."

"Go on."

"The rest of the day actually went really well. We put together snacks, went for a walk, and came back for crafts— stuff they really enjoyed." She smiles, clearly proud of how the day unfolded despite the rocky start. "Tomorrow, I'm thinking of keeping breakfast simple. Maybe cereal," she says with a soft laugh, a hint of playfulness returning to her tone.

Her expression shifts, the lightness in her eyes dimming as she lets out a sigh.."

She goes on.

"But that doesn't excuse what happened this morning. I messed up. I started a damn fire and put the girls' lives in danger. Ms. M wasn't happy, and I get it. I know you both took a chance on me since I don't have much experience, and I'd understand if you decided this wasn't working out."

She finishes, her voice barely above a whisper as she turns her eyes to mine, waiting for my response. I can tell she's bracing herself for whatever comes next, fully expecting the worst.

I pause, letting her words sink in, taking a moment to process everything she's just told me. She's clearly passion- ate, despite the rough start, and that kind of dedication isn't easy to come by.

Finally, I ask, "What do you have planned for tomorrow?"

"Well," she begins, almost hesitantly, "I actually wanted to talk to you about that. I noticed the house is lacking Christmas cheer, and I was wondering if we could do a little decorating—assuming that's okay with you, of course."

I lift a brow, then wait for her to continue.

"I don't know your holiday traditions, so I didn't want to just start hanging up decorations without talking to you first," she adds, her voice sincere. "But, of course, this all assumes I still have a job tomorrow," she finishes, her smile fading a bit as she glances at me.

I look at her, the decision already made long before she finished speaking. Her breath catches, and I can see the tension in her shoulders, the way her hands grip each other as she waits for my decision.

I let the silence hang for just a moment longer, then say, "You still have a job, Willow."

The relief that floods her face is immediate and intense. She visibly relaxes, her body almost sagging with the weight lifted off her. "I do?"

"Yes. You're thoughtful. You didn't just barge in here and start making changes; you considered what's best for the girls and the house. You're good at planning, even if it didn't go perfectly today. You had structure in place, and the girls responded to that. They had a great day because of you, despite the mishap in the kitchen."

I watch as my words sink in, her eyes widening slightly.

"And most importantly, you're already crazy about those girls. That's not something I can teach, and it's not something that can be replaced. I see the way you care about them, and that's what really matters. Mistakes happen, Willow, but it's how you handle them that counts."

She nods, her expression shifting from relief to something more like gratitude, and maybe even a bit of admiration. I can tell she wasn't expecting this outcome.

She looks up at me, gratitude shining in her eyes. "Thank you," she says softly, and then adds with a bit more energy, "You're right—I'm absolutely crazy about the girls," she gushes.

"Giulia's got this incredible imagination," she says, her eyes lighting up. "She comes up with these wild stories, and I get sucked into her little world. And Lucia—oh my God, she's got this quiet determination. She's so focused when she's drawing or working on something, it's like nothing else exists for her at that moment. They're both just amazing."

Every word out of her mouth just confirms what I already knew: She's perfect for this job. The way she talks about them, with so much warmth and affection, it's clear she's not just doing this for a paycheck. She's genuinely invested in their happiness.

When she finally finishes, I lean back, my gaze steady on her. "There were far more experienced nannies who applied for the job. But it was your connection to the girls that clinched it for you. That goes a very, very long way with me, Willow." She nods; I continue. "But I won't tolerate more incidents like what happened in the kitchen. One mistake is understandable. Repeated mistakes, especially when it comes to the girls' safety, are not."

She stiffens, the seriousness of my words sinking in, and nods quickly. "I completely understand," she says, her voice firm and sincere. "It won't happen again."

Her eyes flash with worry. "Anyway, you must've come into the library for some peace and quiet. Sorry for disturbing you." She turns to get her book, her movements graceful, but I catch the slight hesitation in her steps. . "I'll leave you to it."

As she turns to go, I notice the snow starting to fall outside the window, soft and silent. "You don't have to leave," I say, my voice firm.. "But you're under no obligation to stay, either."

She pauses, turning back to look at me., a small smile tugging at her lips. "Are you sure?"

"I don't say things just to be nice, Willow."

She slowly sits down, her gaze never leaving mine, the tension between us shifting into something more comfortable, but no less charged.. I see her settle back into the chair, and I decide to take the next step. "Can I get you a drink from the bar?"

She nods, her eyes still locked on me. "A glass of wine would be nice."

I rise, feeling her eyes on me as I walk to the bar. As I open the wine, she speaks again, this time with a bit more boldness.. "Mind if I ask you a personal question?"

I turn, meeting her gaze with an amused smirk. "Go ahead."

"Have you read many of these books?"

I chuckle, liking the edge in her tone. "If I didn't know better, I'd say you're implying I keep them just for show."

Her eyes flash again, this time sharper.. "That's not what I meant—" she starts, but I can see she's realized I'm just testing her. She quickly clarifies, her tone softening. "It's just that you seem so busy with work, I wonder when you have time to read."

I nod, acknowledging her point as I pour myself a whiskey and a glass of red wine for her. Handing her the wine, I make my way over to the bookshelf, letting my fingers trail over the spines before pulling out *The Count of Monte Cristo* by Alexandre Dumas. I hold it up for her to see.

"This one," I say, my voice steady, "is a favorite of mine. A story of patience, intelligence, and relentless pursuit. A man wronged, who turns every setback into an opportunity, playing the long game with precision."

She listens intently as I talk, her eyes following my every move.. As I speak, memories of my younger days come flooding back—days spent with my nose buried in books, escaping into worlds far removed from my own.

"When I was a boy, I spent every free moment reading," I continue, more to myself than to her. "Books were my refuge, a place where I could sharpen my mind and learn from characters who faced adversity head-on."

I glance back at her, the seriousness returning to my tone.. "I don't have much time to read these days, but I always carve out a little bit of time. Books keep the mind sharp. What exercise does for the body, books do for the brain."

I take a sip of my whiskey, letting the warmth settle before adding, "And in my line of work, I can't afford to have a dull mind."

I offer her my glass, raising it slightly. "Cheers?"

She pauses just before our glasses touch. "What should we drink to?"

"To a very fruitful working relationship."

Our glasses clink softly, the sound somehow more intimate than it should be. I take a sip, letting the whiskey burn its way down, and as I lower my glass, I catch her gaze lingering on me. In that moment, I feel a pull—dangerous, undeniable.

There's something about the way she looks at me, the way she holds herself with both confidence and vulnerability, that makes it hard to remember why I'm supposed to keep my distance.

The firelight flickers across her face, casting shadows that accentuate the curve of her lips and the depth of her eyes.

For a moment, everything else fades—the house, the snow falling outside, the responsibilities waiting in the other room.

All I can focus on is her, and the very, *very* dangerous draw I feel toward her.

CHAPTER 6

"Now you," he says.

I blink, confused. "Now me what?" I ask, taking a sip of the wine, immediately second-guessing whether it's a bad idea to even have a single glass with my boss.

The way he's looking at me, the effect he has on me—my body's reacting way too intensely, and I can already feel a hot, wet ache pooling between my legs just from being this close to him.

"I want you to tell me one of your favorite books," he says, his eyes flicking down to the mystery novel on the armrest.my book. "I enjoy a good light read every now and then."

My cheeks flush, embarrassed by my choice. "I don't normally read stuff like this," I admit, trying to play it off. "I just wanted something mindless."

He watches me closely, and I feel a little exposed, like he can see right through my excuses. Needing to distract myself, I get up and head to the bookshelf, scanning the spines.

As I run my fingers over the titles, I think about the steamy books I actually love—the ones I devour when I'm alone. . The ones with scandalous plots and steamy scenes that make my heart race. There's no way in hell I'm telling him about *those*.

I keep searching, trying to find something that won't give too much away, all the while hyper-aware of him standing behind me, watching my every move, my skin tingling under his gaze.

I reach for *Pride and Prejudice* by Jane Austen, a classic that always hits the spot. Holding it up, I turn to him.

He arches an eyebrow, intrigued. "Why that one?" he asks.

I smile, feeling a bit more confident now. "I read this when I was a girl, and it changed my life. Elizabeth Bennet is every-thing—smart, witty, and not afraid to stand up for herself. She's got this fire in her that I've always admired. Plus, the banter between her and Mr. Darcy? Iconic. It showed me that you can be strong and still have a soft spot for romance."

I'm getting carried away, the passion in my voice growing as I continue. "It's like, as a girl, you're sometimes taught to be quiet, to be nice, but this book showed me that being strong and outspoken isn't something to be ashamed of. It's some-thing to embrace."

I'm completely lost in the memory of how much this story shaped me. "It made me see that you can be both strong and soft, that you don't have to choose. You can be passionate and still care deeply about people. It was a game-changer for me."

For a moment, I'm in my own world, reliving the impact this book had on me, completely forgetting where I am and who I'm with.

When I finally snap back to reality, I glance over at Nico. He's staring at me, silent and intense. I raise an eyebrow. "What?"

He gives a small, almost amused smile. "I was just enjoying listening to you talk."

My cheeks heat up, and I laugh nervously. "I tend to ramble when I'm nervous."

He leans in slightly, his gaze still locked on mine. "Why are you nervous?"

I hesitate, feeling the tension rise between us. "Well, my boss is standing right here," I say, trying to keep it light, though the thought in my head is much more explicit: *While I'm barely wearing anything.* But I keep that part to myself, biting my lip as the air between us thickens with unspoken words..

He's still watching me, his eyes dark and hungry, like he's ready to devour me right here and now. My heart skips a beat, and I feel a strange blend of nerves and arousal swirling in my stomach. I'm starting to think I should get out of here *now*, before I do something I might regret—something I know I shouldn't want as much as I do.

He finishes his whiskey in one smooth motion, his gaze dropping to my half-empty glass. "Need a top up?" he asks, his voice low and smooth.

I nod, unable to trust my voice as I hand him the glass. He walks to the bar, and I stare at his ass in those perfectly tailored slacks, the way they hug every inch of his body. My mind is racing with thoughts I shouldn't be having about my boss, but I can't seem to stop myself.

He returns, leaning casually against the bookshelf, his presence commanding the room. He hands me the glass, and I take it, trying to steady my shaky hands.

"You know," he says, "his voice rich and velvety, "I could listen to you talk about books all night."

Before I can think, I blurt out, "Well, there are other things we could do all night."

As soon as the words leave my mouth, I feel my face flush with embarrassment, realizing how that must have sounded.

His grin widens, that sexy-as-fuck, predatory look flashing in his eyes again. He leans in closer, his breath warm against my skin. "Oh? And what else could we do all night, Willow?" he asks, his voice a seductive whisper that sends shivers down my spine.

My body reacts before my mind can catch up, and I know I'm in deep trouble.

He leans in so close I can smell the whiskey on his breath, the warm, smoky scent mixing with the heat radiating off his body.

"I think you know what I mean," I murmur softly, the words slipping out before I can stop them. It's like my desire for him has completely taken over, pushing me to the point of no return.

His eyes darken, and I know he gets the message loud and clear. He moves even closer, closing the distance between us, and then his lips are on mine.

The kiss is intense., a heady mix of urgency and heat. His lips are firm, demanding, and he tastes like whiskey and something darker. It's intoxicating.

His body presses against mine, solid and strong, and I can feel every inch of him. The warmth of his chest against me, the strength in his arms as they wrap around me—it's overwhelming in the best possible way. I'm lost in the moment, completely consumed by the way he's kissing me, how he's pulling me deeper into this irresistible heat between us.

I moan into his mouth, the sound escaping before I can think to hold it back. I'm soaked through my panties, every nerve in my body on fire as his big, strong hands grip my hips, pulling me against him with a possessive intensity.

I know, without a doubt, that I want to lose my virginity to him right here, right now. I can't help it; I've never wanted anyone this badly in my life.

We kiss long and deep, like we're both starving for it, and I can't get enough. Then his hands slide under my shirt, and when he takes hold of my breasts, electricity shoots through me.

His hands are big, rough, and when he kneads my flesh, it sets my whole body on fire. My nipples harden instantly, so sensitive that every little movement he makes sends waves of pleasure through me. I can't hold back the moan that escapes my lips, feeling like I might actually come from this alone.

He pulls back just enough to grin down at me, that wicked look in his eyes driving me wild.

"I can tell you like it when I touch you like this," he says, his voice low and teasing, dripping with confidence.

"I love it," I breathe out, my voice shaky with need.

His hardness presses against me, and all I can think about is how much I want him, how much I need more. I push my hips against him, craving the feel of him. I slowly place my hand on his cock through his slacks. It's a bold move, one I've never made before.

As I stroke him through the fabric, feeling his hardness beneath my fingers, Nico growls like an animal, the sound low and primal. It sends sparks through my blood, only making me want him more. His reaction fuels my desire, pushing me to keep going, to take things further than I ever have before.

In one swift motion, he pulls my shirt off, leaving my upper body bare before him. The cool air hits my skin, but the heat between us burns even hotter. His eyes darken with lust as he takes me in, and then he leans down, his mouth finding my nipples. He kisses them, his lips warm and wet, before he starts licking and sucking, each pull of his mouth sending jolts of pleasure through me.

I keep stroking him, my hand moving with more confidence now as his mouth works magic on my breasts. The sensation is almost too much, and I find myself arching into him, moaning as I feel the pressure building inside me, ready to explode at any moment.

He lifts his mouth from my tits, his eyes locking onto mine with a smoldering intensity that makes my knees weak.

"You taste so fucking good," he murmurs, his voice low and rough, sending a shiver straight down my spine. "I can't wait to make you scream my name. I'm going to take you right here, make you come so hard you won't be able to think straight."

His words are like fire spreading through my body. My breath catches, and before I can even process it, his hand is sliding down the front of my shorts, fingers slipping under the fabric to find my drenched pussy. The moment he touches me, I gasp, a moan slipping out as I instinctively buck into his hand, desperate for more..

He smirks, his fingers teasing me, sliding through the wetness that's already soaked my panties. "You're so fucking wet for me," he growls. "So turned on."

I bite my lower lip, closing my eyes as I focus on the way he's touching me.. His fingers are skilled, confident, moving in slow, deliberate circles that drive me wild. He knows exactly where to press, where to rub, how to tease me until I'm on the edge of losing control.

I try to talk dirty back to him, but the words come out a little awkward. "I... I want you to... to make me come," I stammer, my voice shaky with desire. He chuckles, and I instantly feel my face heat up with embarrassment. "I'm sorry," I mumble, biting my lip. "I'm not exactly good at this."

He smirks, his fingers still working their magic on me. "Every fucking word out of your mouth is turning me on," he says, his voice thick with lust.

His touch is relentless, his fingers moving in a way that makes my toes curl. I love how he's taking control, guiding me, pushing me closer and closer to the edge. The pressure inside me builds, and I'm so close, right on the brink of an orgasm that's going to shatter me.

He holds me there, teasing, pulling back just enough to drive me crazy. My breath comes in ragged gasps, my body trembling as I try to hold on.

"What do you want, Willow?" he asks, his voice low and demanding.

"I want to come," I pant, my voice barely a whisper.

He grins, clearly enjoying the way I'm practically begging for it. "Say please."

"Please," I moan, the word spilling out before I can think.. " Please, Mr. Conti, I need to come."

His fingers push inside me, his thumb pressing down on my clit, and I'm done. The orgasm slams into me like a tidal wave, so intense it feels like I'm floating out of my own body. My entire world narrows down to the pleasure pulsing through me—wave after wave of heat and ecstasy, making my vision blur and my breath catch..

My legs tremble uncontrollably, and it's like every nerve in my body is on fire. I'm gripping onto him like he's the only thing keeping me from floating away. I'm lost in it, completely undone, and for a second, I don't even know where I am.

As the orgasm starts to fade, my body finally begins to settle, but instead of feeling satisfied, I'm surprised by how much more I want him. The release intensified everything—I'm even more desperate for him now.

Standing there, still trembling, I know this is it. This is the moment I've been waiting for, whether I knew it or not—the moment I lose my virginity, and to him.

"What do you want, Willow?" he asks again, his voice low and full of promise.

The words spill out of me, no hesitation. "I want you inside me."

His grin is wicked, knowing. He pulls down my shorts in one smooth motion, stripping me bare. His lips follow, kissing every inch of me—my breasts, my stomach, down to my pussy. He's not just touching me; he's worshiping me, and it's driving me wild.

Then he scoops me up effortlessly, like I weigh nothing, and carries me to the table—the very one I'd fantasized about. He lays me down, the cool wood sending a shiver up my spine.

When he pulls off his shirt, revealing those hard muscles, I can barely breathe.

God, he looks so fucking good.

My eyes drift down to his cock, and holy shit—it's thick, long, and glistening at the tip. Just the sight of it makes me squirm with pleasure, heat pooling between my legs all over again. But a tiny part of me hesitates, wondering if it's too big, too much for my first time.

For a split second, I consider telling him. Should I let him know that I'm a virgin? Maybe he needs to, maybe he'd take things slower. But what if he stops? What if this perfect moment slips away? I can't let that happen—I don't want him to stop.

Before I can overthink it, he leans over me, his body hovering above mine, and I feel the head of his cock graze my lips. My breath hitches, and the anticipation nearly drives me crazy.

"Protection," he says.

Shit. Right.

"I could go grab something..." he offers.

"I'm on the pill," I reply. It's not a lie. I've been on birth control since I was fifteen for acne. A little ironic for a twenty-three-year-old virgin, but there it is.

He grins, pleased there will be no interruption to our fun. "You ready?"

"Yes," I whisper.

He positions himself at my entrance, and as he starts to push in gently, the sensation is like nothing I've ever felt before. There's a stretch, a pressure that's both strange and incredibly intense, and my body instinctively tightens around him.

It's a mix of discomfort and pleasure, the fullness over-whelming as he slowly fills me inch by inch. The initial pain fades into something deeper, more raw, as my body adjusts to him, and I feel myself opening up to him in a way I've never thought possible.

He starts to move inside me, slow and steady, and I'm completely transfixed by everything about him. The way his muscles tense and flex with every thrust, the sheen of sweat glistening on his skin, and that intoxicating mix of his scent —musky, masculine, with just a hint of the whiskey he drank earlier.

His eyes are dark and intense, locked onto mine, and it feels like he's completely focused on me, like I'm the only thing that matters right now.

I wrap my legs around his hips, pulling him closer, and the movement drives him deeper.

"You like that, don't you?" he growls, his voice dripping with lust as he bottoms out, filling me so completely I can't believe I actually fit all of him inside me. The fullness is overwhelming, but in the best way possible.

"Fuck, yes," I gasp, the words slipping out before I can stop them. He grins, clearly enjoying my desperation.

His lips crash into mine in a deep, hungry kiss, his tongue teasing mine as he moves. "You're so damn tight," he murmurs against my lips, the heat in his voice sending shivers down my spine. I'm lost in the sensation of him—his warmth, his strength, the raw intensity that makes every nerve in my body light up.

"Take me harder," I whisper, my voice shaky but full of need. He obliges, thrusting harder, and the tight sting from before starts to fade, replaced by a building pleasure that makes my toes curl.

"God, you feel amazing," he groans.

I can't help the moans that slip out, the way my body responds to his every thrust. It doesn't take long before I'm there again, the orgasm crashing over me, more intense than I ever imagined. My body clenches around him as I cry out into his mouth, completely lost in the pleasure he's giving me.

He pulls out slowly, and I see his gaze drop to where we were just connected. There's a tinge of blood, and his eyes go wide.

"Are you a virgin?" he asks, shock bracing his voice.

A bashful grin spreads on my face.

"I was."

CHAPTER 7

NICO

Without thinking, I grab a tissue from the nearby desk and clean myself off, my mind still reeling. When I turn back to her, I'm struck by how insanely sexy she looks laid out on the table—completely naked, her legs still spread from where I just had her. Her skin is flushed, a soft sheen of sweat glistening on her toned body. Her breasts are full, nipples still hard from my touch, and the curve of her waist flows perfectly into the swell of her hips. Every inch of her is pure temptation, and all I can think about is being back inside her.

But the fact that she was a virgin is a shock.

"Why didn't you tell me?"

She meets my gaze, biting her lip, and then says, "I thought it might make things awkward and make you want to stop."

I pause, taking in her words. . She's got a point. "You're right. I would've wanted to make your first time more special."

She shakes her head, giving me a look that's both determined and a little playful. "It was special. For me, at least." Her words hang in the air, full of certainty. Then she asks, a challenge in her eyes, "Do *you* want to stop?"

I chuckle, the sound low and full of desire. "Hell, no," I say, moving closer, my hand sliding up her thigh. "Stopping is the last thing I want."

I'm still hard as hell, the need to be inside her again almost overwhelming. I want to make her come again and again, to show her just how good this can be.

"Good. I want more. I want everything."

"Come down from there," I command. "And get on all fours."

She obeys, moving down onto the floor, her body gliding gracefully as she gets into position. She glances back at me with an impossibly sexy look, her eyes full of anticipation and desire. The sight of her naked and ready on all fours, her ass perfectly round and inviting, sends a fresh wave of lust crashing through me.

Her back arches beautifully, and I take a moment to appreciate every curve of her body, from the dip of her waist to the roundness of her hips, the way her wetness glistens between her legs.

I move behind her, dropping to my knees and positioning myself at her entrance. "Are you ready?" I ask, my voice thick with need.

She nods, her voice breathless. "Yes."

I slowly enter her, filling her inch by inch, the tightness of her body gripping me in a way that's almost too good to handle.

I start slow, thrusting into her from behind, savoring the way her pussy grips me with every movement. Her body adjusts, her moans growing louder as I build speed, and the sound is pure music to my ears. I lean over her, my hands gripping her hips, pulling her back onto me with every thrust.

The sound of my balls slapping against her ripe ass turns me on even more.

"You feel so fucking good, Willow," I growl, my voice thick with desire. "So tight. I could do this all night."

She moans in response, her confidence growing as she pushes back against me, meeting my rhythm. Her body is perfect—her ass bouncing with every thrust, her back arching beautifully, and her skin flushed with pleasure. Her moans turn into needy whimpers, and I know she's getting close again.

"I want you to come for me," I command, my voice deep and authoritative.. " Now."

Her breath hitches, and then she's there, her body tightening around me as she comes, her back arching as waves of pleasure ripple through her. The sight of her losing herself to the orgasm, her body shaking and her moans spilling out uncontrollably, almost pushes me over the edge, but I hold back. I'm not done with her yet.

As she recovers, I flip her over onto her back, positioning myself above her. I don't waste a second—I thrust back into her, hard and deep, capturing her lips in a hungry kiss. My tongue invades her mouth, and she moans into me, her hands gripping my shoulders as I take control again. Every part of her is mine, and I'm going to make sure she knows it.

I slide into her again and again, this time slow and deep, letting her feel every inch of me. Her eyes widen, her lips parting in a soft gasp as I fill her completely.

I lean in close, my voice a low growl in her ear. "You like that? You like how deep I'm going?" I ask, my breath hot against her skin.

"Yes," she breathes, her voice full of need.

I keep the rhythm slow, deliberate, teasing her with every thrust. "I want to come inside you, Willow. You want that?"

She nods, her eyes dark with desire. "I want to come with you. One more time."

I grip her hips, angling myself just right, bringing her to the edge again. Her moans become desperate, her nails digging into my back as I push her closer and closer to the brink. When I feel her tightening around me, right at that peak, I let go, thrusting deep and hard as she falls over the edge.

The sensation of her coming around me, her body clenching in rhythmic waves, is enough to send me into my own release. I come hard, the pleasure hitting me like a freight train, hot and intense.

Every pulse of her orgasm pulls me deeper, and I feel myself emptying inside her, the connection between us more raw and real than anything I've ever experienced.

We finish together, bodies trembling, breath mingling. When it's over, I scoop her up, holding her close, her body fitting perfectly against mine. She curls up next to me, her head resting on my chest, and I can't help but notice how strangely *right* it all feels. As if this is exactly where we're both meant to be.

We lay there in silence for a while, her body warm and soft against mine. I'm torn, my mind running wild. I love the way she feels, the way she looks nestled against me, and the sex... it was fucking incredible.

I know, even now, that the memory of her underneath me, her eyes full of desire, is something that'll be burned into my mind forever.

She shifts, rolling onto her side to face me. "What are you thinking?" she asks, her voice soft but curious, pulling me from my thoughts.

I've got a lot on my mind, more than I care to admit, but I'm not about to spill everything right now.

"I just can't believe you're a virgin," I say, correcting myself quickly. "I mean, *were* a virgin."

She raises an eyebrow, intrigued. "Why's that?"

I look her over, taking in every detail. "Well, you're stunning. You must've had your pick of interested boys since high school."

She lets out a small, almost self-conscious laugh.She laughs. "It's complicated. High school wasn't exactly glamorous for me. I was awkward and gawky—no confidence at all. That's actually why I got into yoga, to develop a little grace."

I run my hand down her side, appreciating the lithe, toned body that yoga has clearly given her. "You have," I say, my voice firm, leaving no room for doubt.."

She blushes at the compliment, and I find myself loving that blush more and more every time I see it.

"I had some boyfriends here and there, but none of them were really that exciting. Truth be told, I only dated them because it felt like I was supposed to. You know, just going through the motions." She pauses, her eyes flicking up to meet mine.

"And none of them ever piqued your sexual interest?"

She smirks, not missing a beat. "Well, clearly, I was just waiting for the right one. And I finally found it." Her confidence is infectious, and I can't resist leaning in to kiss her, hard and possessive. She melts into it, responding just as fiercely. She pulls back, her eyes sparkling. "I finished my degree last year and didn't do the whole college experience. Casual sex seemed to be an important part of that."

Her words give me pause. I'd almost forgotten how young she is. At least twenty years my junior. I feel a cold knot forming in my gut. I sit up, the weight of what we've just done pressing down on me. This isn't right.

She notices the change in my demeanor, and I can see the concern in her eyes.. But I can't shake the feeling that I've crossed a line I can't uncross.

I stand up, leaving her on the floor as I grab my clothes and step over to the fire, staring into the flames. The heat radiates from it, but it doesn't do anything to thaw the cold knot tightening in my chest. I can feel her eyes on me, the weight of her silence pressing against my back.

"What happened?" she finally asks, her voice shaky. "Did I say something wrong?"

I take a few more moments, still gathering my thoughts, before I finally turn to face her. "I'm sorry," I say, my voice firm but laced with regret.

"Sorry?" she repeats, confusion and hurt flashing in her eyes.

"That's right," I reply, my tone clipped as I start to pull on my clothes. "I'm glad you enjoyed it, but this... it was wrong. I'm not just your boss—I'm nearly twice your age. This never should've happened."

She's stunned, her mouth opening and closing as she tries to process my words. "But I wanted it to happen," she stammers, clearly not understanding why I'm pulling away.

"Regardless," I say, buttoning my shirt with finality, "it won't happen again." My voice is steady, even as the weight of the decision bears down on me.

I finish dressing, straightening my clothes as if to put everything back in order, as if that could somehow undo what we've done. "You're welcome to spend time in the library," I tell her, the distance in my voice unmistakable.. "But tomorrow, our professional relationship will resume."

She's still sitting there, naked and shocked, unable to comprehend how things turned so quickly. But I can't afford to let this go any further. I turn and leave the room, shutting the door behind me, sealing off what can never be undone..

I make my way up to my room, each step heavier than the last. I feel like a total asshole—what the hell was I thinking, sleeping with an employee? Hell, she's practically fresh out of college. The thought alone makes my stomach churn.

I strip off my clothes, letting them fall carelessly to the floor. I head straight for my private stash of whiskey, pouring myself a generous nightcap. The burn of the alcohol as it slides down my throat is a welcome distraction, but it doesn't do much to dull the guilt gnawing at my insides.

I stare out the window, watching the snow fall, the silence of the night doing nothing to quiet the storm in my mind.

I chastise myself for taking advantage of her. I'm supposed to be the responsible one, the adult who knows better. She's young, still figuring out life, and I should've known better. This can't happen again. It won't. But no matter how much I try to convince myself, the images from earlier keep flashing through my mind.

Her body arching beneath me, the way she moaned my name, the feeling of her tightness as I pushed inside her for the first time. The look in her eyes as she came, the way her lips parted in pleasure—each memory more vivid than the last....

I grip the glass tighter, realizing with a sinking feeling that moving on from what happened tonight is going to be the challenge of a lifetime.. Tonight isIt's already burned into my mind, and I'm not sure how I'm going to forget it—or if I even want to.

CHAPTER 8

What the hell just happened?

I throw on my clothes, each movement sharp and angry, the sting of his rejection still fresh.

I'm totally pissed off, my emotions a mess. I plop down into the chair, snatch up my glass of wine, and take a long, frustrated sip. The events of the last hour keep replaying in my mind, and I can't make sense of the boiling conflict inside me.

On one hand, I'm proud of myself. I finally took control of my sexuality, made my own damn choice, and did it with a man I genuinely wanted. No more waiting around for the "right time" or the "right guy"—I decided for myself, and it was liberating.

But then there's Nico's reaction, and that's what's really messing me up. The way he pulled away, the guilt in his eyes, like I was some kid he shouldn't have touched. I feel confused, hurt, and, if I'm being honest, a little embarrassed. Did I push too hard?

I thought I was taking a step toward something empowering, but now I'm questioning everything. Did he regret it the moment it happened? And if he did, what does that say about me? Was I just some stupid, impulsive girl who got in over her head?

I take another sip of wine, the taste bitter on my tongue as the questions swirl around in my head, each one cutting deeper than the last.

I'm bouncing back and forth between feeling like a total badass and like the biggest idiot on the planet. One minute, I'm replaying the way his hands felt on me, the way his fingers teased me until I was practically begging for more. The memory of him inside me, slow and deep, making me come over and over, and I can still hear the way he growled my name, like I was the only thing that mattered in the world at that moment.

God, it was so hot—every single second of it.

But then, doubt creeps in. Did I misread the whole situation? Was I completely naive to think I could handle a casual encounter with someone like him—older, more experienced, and clearly way out of my league?

I can't help but worry that I've not only screwed up my job but also thrown my self-respect out the window. I've never been one for meaningless flings, and I was so careful about my first time, wanting it to be special. And it was... wasn't it? I can't shake the feeling that maybe I rushed into something I wasn't ready for.

. . .

I need to figure out what I really want—what this all means for me—but right now, all I've got is a mess of emotions and no clear answers.

I decide there's one thing I can do right now—find out more about my boss. Who the hell is he, really? I hurry over to the bar, topping off my glass. With my wine in hand, I head to my room and grab my laptop, a sense of determination fueling my every step. .

I type his name into the search bar and hit enter, not entirely sure what I'm expecting to find. But when the results pop up, I nearly spit out my wine. There are tons of articles, all with his name plastered across them, and not in the way I expected.

I read the words "Conti Family Syndicate." What the actual fuck? My eyes widen as I click on one of the headlines, my heart racing. The article talks about him having a business that looks totally legit on the surface, but the article dives into all these rumors and allegations about him being the head of a damn *Mob family*. Is this for real?

I scroll through more articles, each one more intense than the last.. Words like "organized crime," "underworld connections," and "Mafia" jump out at me.

My mind is spinning. How did I miss this? The man who just took my virginity might be a freaking mob boss? I take another big gulp of wine, trying to wrap my head around what I'm seeing.

I furiously scroll through articles, trying to piece together what I can, but it's all so damn murky. Some sources hint that he's the boss, while others suggest he's just a front man for something bigger. Nothing is clear, and it's driving me nuts.

Who is Nico Conti, really? And what the hell have I gotten myself into?

Frustrated, I slam my MacBook shut and fall back onto the bed, letting out an exasperated sigh. I'm still practically buzzing from the sex, and even though I know it's a terrible idea, I want him again. The memory of his hands on my body, the way he took control, how he filled me so completely—it's all I can think about.

I close my eyes, letting those memories wash over me. I can still feel the way he moved inside me, the way his muscles tensed with every thrust, the low growl of his voice in my ear as he pushed me closer to the edge. The way he looked at me, like he was hungry for more, and the way he made me feel—so wanted, so alive, so completely his in that moment.

A big, stupid smile spreads across my face as I relive every delicious detail. Despite everything, despite the confusion and chaos, I can't deny how incredible it was.

As I drift off to sleep, those memories play like a highlight reel in my mind, and I'm left with one delicious thought: I want him again.

~

It's early Saturday morning, and I'm stepping into the home gym at the Conti estate just in time for sunrise—the perfect time for yoga.

NANNY FOR THE DON | 63

One of the perks of this job is access to this gym. It has everything you could possibly want—weights, cardio machines, and a huge open, matted space just begging for a good stretch session.

The view is the cherry on top—a stunning snowy garden that looks like something out of a movie. It's serene, and just what I need to clear my head after the craziness of last night. I set up my laptop on a bench, ready to film some yoga content to edit for YouTube later.

I hit record on my camera, flashing a smile at the lens. "Good morning, yogis! Today, we're kicking off with a sunrise flow to wake up the body and clear the mind. Perfect for those frosty mornings when you need a little extra warmth from within."

I step onto the mat, taking a deep breath. "We'll start with some gentle stretches to get the blood flowing, then move into a dynamic Vinyasa sequence to really build some heat. Think lots of sun salutations, warrior poses, and a killer core sequence to finish it off. By the end of this session, you'll feel energized, grounded, and ready to tackle whatever the day throws at you."

I move into a gentle cat-cow stretch, feeling the tension in my back start to melt away. "Grab your mat, find a comfy spot, and let's flow together."

I go through my routine, starting with a few deep breaths and some gentle stretches.

But as I go through the poses, my mind drifts back to Nico, the memory of his hands on my body, the way he looked at me with that intense gaze. A rush of heat spreads through me, and I find myself biting my lower lip in arousal, totally distracted. My focus slips, and before I know it, I'm wobbling right out of Warrior pose, toppling into a heap on the mat.

"Ugh," I groan., sighing at my clumsiness. "Guess I'll have to edit that little tumble out later." I shake it off and get back into position, pushing through the rest of my routine, even as thoughts of my boss linger at the edges of my mind..

As I finish, I close my eyes and imagine my future—a cute little studio in the West Village, a business that's all mine. Yoga wouldn't just be a hobby anymore; it'd be my life.

When I'm done, I close my laptop, feeling good and limber, even if my mind is still half lost in a certain someone. I jump onto the treadmill for a quick burst of cardio, just enough to get my heart pumping.

As I'm hitting my stride, my phone alarm goes off, snapping me back to reality. Almost time to get the girls up and the day started. I slow down, reaching for my phone to silence the alarm, but another chime interrupts me—this one's a message from Ms. M.

Mr. Conti gave the OK for Christmas decor, it reads. *You can drive the girls wherever you need to get it.*

A grin spreads across my face. The whole situation is complicated, no doubt, but at least I've got something fun to focus on today. I hop off the treadmill, practically bouncing with excitement as I head into the private shower. The warm water cascades over me, washing away the sweat and lingering tension from my workout..

Maybe I can turn this insane situation into something halfway normal.

CHAPTER 9

I'm driving through the quiet Sunday morning streets of Manhattan, the city barely waking up as I navigate through the familiar routes.barely up.

Fatigue weighs heavily on me, a consequence of the long, grueling day before. I'd spent most of it chasing down leads, trying to get to the bottom of my father's murder. The frustration of it all is a constant throb at the back of my skull, and no amount of coffee or determination seems to dull it.

As I'm lost in thought, my phone buzzes. I glance at the screen before answering, recognizing the name instantly. Salvatore "Sal" Mancini. One of the few men I trust in this whole mess.

"What've you got for me, Sal?" I ask, my voice steady despite the turmoil inside.

"Not much, boss," Sal responds. ", a hint of frustration in his tone. "We've been shaking down every contact we've got, but nothing new has come up. It's like everyone's gone deaf, dumb, and blind overnight."

I grip the steering wheel tighter, anger simmering just below the surface. "It's insane, Sal. My father gets taken out, and there's no word on the street? Not a damn whisper?"

"Yeah, it all stinks to high heaven," Sal agrees, his voice laced with the same frustration I'm feeling.. "It's like someone's got the whole city under their thumb, keeping this thing quiet."

I exhale sharply, the pieces of the puzzle refusing to fit together. Someone out there knows what happened, and I won't stop until I find them.

Sal's going over potential plans, laying out the options in that methodical way of his, but my focus drifts the moment I pull up to my townhouse. The front of the place is completely transformed—decked out in the most tasteful Christmas decor I've ever seen..

Twinkling white lights wrap around the columns and railings, casting a warm glow across the fresh layer of snow that's just beginning to fall, like something straight out of a holiday movie. Wreaths with red bows hang perfectly on each window, and garlands are draped over the front door, their evergreen branches dotted with pinecones and holly berries.

It's the kind of thing that shouldn't get to me, but it does. There's something almost too perfect about it, too serene compared to the chaos in my life.

"Boss, you still there?" Sal's voice cuts through my thoughts, pulling me back to the conversation.

"Yeah," I mutter., shaking my head as if to clear it. "We'll talk later, Sal."

I end the call and pull into the private garage on the lowest level. The snow's still falling softly as I step out of the car, but my mind's already on the interior of the house. I take the elevator up to the first floor, and as the doors open, I'm greeted by the same level of holiday perfection inside.

The halls are lined with more garlands, each one more intricate than the last, with shimmering ornaments and delicate fairy lights. Every surface is adorned with something festive—candles, miniature reindeer, and perfectly placed poinsettias.

It's warm, inviting, and just as stunning as the exterior. I take a deep breath, letting the scene sink in as I step further inside, my tension momentarily melting away.

As I head toward the den, I'm stopped in my tracks by the sound of excited little voices. Giulia and Lucia come barreling in, their faces lit up with pure joy as they rush to greet me. They throw their tiny arms around my legs, nearly knocking me off balance. I smile at them, the weight of the morning's stress lifting as I lean down to kiss each of their foreheads.

"Papa!" they squeal in unison, their eyes sparkling with excitement.

"Hey, my little angels," I greet them warmly, ruffling their hair. Their joy is contagious, and for a moment, the darkness of the past few days fades into the background.

Olivia enters the room, her presence bringing me back to reality. As much as I'm focused on my girls, I can't help but scan the room for Willow.

"Where's Willow?"

Olivia raises an eyebrow, a knowing look in her eyes that suggests she's already pieced together more than I'd like. "She has Sundays off, remember? But I believe she's down in the gym."

Before I can respond, the girls are tugging at my hands, their excitement bubbling over. "Papa, come see the tree! You have to see it!" Giulia insists, pulling me toward the den.

The twins tug me into the den, and the sight that greets me is nothing short of breathtaking. The Christmas tree stands tall and majestic, its branches full and perfectly shaped. Twinkling lights weave through the greenery, casting a soft, magical glow that dances across the room. Ornaments of every kind hang from the branches—glass baubles, delicate snowflakes, and handmade decorations that add a personal touch. The star at the top shines brightly, completing the picture-perfect scene.

The fire crackles in the fireplace, filling the den with a warmth that makes the room feel inviting in a way it usually isn't.

"Papa, look!" Giulia's voice pulls me out of my thoughts as she proudly holds up an ornament. It's simple but beautiful —a picture of the three of us, framed in a little wreath she clearly made herself. The sight of it hits me harder than I expected, and I feel a lump form in my throat.

"We went tree shopping with Miss Willow and Ms. M!" Lucia chimes in, her voice filled with excitement.in. "And we got all the ornaments and decorations!"

"Then we made Christmas cookies with Miss Willow last night!" Giulia adds, practically bouncing on her toes.

Olivia winks at me. "And don't worry, Mr. Conti—there was no fire this time."

The girls are still bouncing with excitement, their energy seemingly endless. "Ms. M, can we go to the park and play in the snow?" Lucia asks, her eyes wide with anticipation.

Olivia smiles, always patient with them. "Yes, of course."

Giulia turns to me. , her face lit up with hope. "Papa, will you come with us?"

I kneel down to their level, my hands resting on their small shoulders. "I'd love to, but I have some things I need to finish first." Their faces fall with disappointment, and it tugs at something deep inside me.. "But I promise," I add, my tone firm and sincere,, "as soon as you get back, the rest of the day is ours. We'll do whatever you want."

That promise seems to satisfy them, and they both nod eagerly. "Okay, Papa!" they chime together.

Olivia gathers them up and they head out, leaving me standing alone in the den. I take a deep breath, trying to shake off the lingering guilt, and head into the kitchen. There, I start making a pre-workout shake, reminding myself that I haven't had any gym time lately. That needs to change. First, a workout, then work.

I change into my workout clothes and make my way downstairs. As I reach the gym, I remember Olivia mentioned Willow was down here. I push open the door, and the sight that greets me stops me in my tracks.

Willow is in the middle of a yoga pose, her body perfectly aligned, every muscle engaged. The sheer grace of her movement, the way her leggings cling to every curve, leaves me thunderstruck. I stand there, unable to look away, my breath catching in my throat.

I hear Willow's voice, clear and confident. She's facing away from me, her attention focused on her open laptop. I glance at the screen and see a grid of little squares, each one showing someone in their own space, following along. It hits me—she's teaching a virtual class.

I hold the door open, letting her words wash over me.

"Alright, everyone, let's finish strong," she says, her tone encouraging and upbeat. "Move into your final Warrior II, really ground yourself through your feet. Feel that strength, that power in your legs. We're wrapping up with some deep, calming stretches, so take this time to focus on your breath."

She flows into the next pose, her movements fluid and graceful, like she was made for this.

I stand in the doorway, watching her lithe body as she moves seamlessly from one pose to the next, her skin-tight workout clothes clinging to every curve. The way her muscles flex and stretch is mesmerizing, each movement drawing me in more than I'd like to admit.

I can't tear my eyes away from her, the sight of her stretching before me igniting something primal deep inside.. My cock pulses to life, responding instantly to the sight of her. The temptation to step inside and make my presence known is almost too much to resist, but I force myself to stay put, letting the desire simmer just beneath the surface.

I watch as she moves from position to position, each transition seamless, filled with poise and ease. Her body is a work of art, even more beautiful in motion. The way those yoga pants hug her ass, showing off every curve, makes it impossible to look away. Her tank top clings to her in all the right places, highlighting the gentle swell of her breasts, the curve of her waist leading down to those full, sexy-as-fuck hips. She's graceful, almost like a dancer, every movement deliberate and skilled.

I know I shouldn't be staring, eyeing her like she's a piece of meat, but damn it, I can't help myself. Something about her draws me in and makes it impossible to pretend I'm unaffected.

My mind flashes back to Friday night in the library, the way she felt beneath me, the way she responded to every touch. I'd told her we needed to put it behind us, that it was a mistake, but right now, standing here watching her, it's hard as hell to convince myself.

I want her. It's that simple, that primal. Even though I know better, even though I've tried to push it out of my mind, the desire lingers, simmering just beneath the surface. And as much as I hate to admit it, it's getting harder and harder to pretend I don't want her again.

I'm not the kind of man who constantly lusts after women half my age. But something about Willow pulls me in, making it harder to keep my distance. It's not just her body —though God knows that's part of it—it's the way she carries herself.

I listen as she wraps up the lesson, her voice calm and professional. "Alright, everyone, great job today! Does anyone have any questions before we finish?"

As I watch her answer the questions like a pro, I push the thought of how sexy she looks doing those poses out of my mind. I remind myself that she's incredibly talented, knowledgeable, and deserves more respect than to be ogled like this.

But as she closes the laptop and stretches one more time, her body arching in a way that makes my heart pound, I realize I'm at a crossroads. I could shut the door and walk away, leave things as they are. Or I could step inside, make my presence known, and see where it leads.

The decision doesn't take long. I open the door wider and step inside.

CHAPTER 10

I let out a little yelp when I see Nico stepping inside. I'd been so caught up in my post-yoga stretch that I hadn't even noticed him until he was right there, looking all brooding and intense.

"Morning," he greets me, his voice deep and calm, like he didn't just sneak up on me.

At first, I'm totally taken by the sight of him. He's wearing gym shorts that show off his powerful legs, and a sleeveless shirt that exposes those thick, juicy arms that make my mouth go dry. My pussy clenches at the sight of him, a reminder of just how much I want him despite everything.

But I push past it—no way am I letting him get to me like that again. Still a little irked by the way he acted Friday night in the library, I start gathering my things, trying to keep my cool.

"I'll get out of your way," I say, my tone a bit sharp. I'm not about to let him think he can just waltz in here and throw me off my game.

I shove my laptop into my bag, avoiding his gaze as I grab my water bottle and towel. The whole time, I'm hyper-aware of him standing there watching me, but I refuse to let it rattle me. If he thinks he can just walk in and expect things to go back to normal after Friday night, he's got another thing coming.

I turn to face him, watching as he moves closer and closer, a hungry, lustful look in his eyes. I know that look—it's the same one he had the other night when he practically pounced on me.

I try to tell him I know what he's thinking and that it's a really bad idea. "Mr. Conti, I know what you're—"

Before I can even finish the sentence, he closes the gap between us and kisses me, hard. His lips crash against mine, shutting me up instantly, and every coherent thought I had flies right out the window.

The logical part of my brain is screaming at me to stop this, that I should tell him no, but every other part of me wants nothing more than to give in to him. His mouth is demanding, and the way he's kissing me makes me feel like I'm the only thing he wants in the entire world.

Screw it, I think, letting go of whatever resistance I had left. I melt into the kiss, wrapping my arms around his neck and pulling him closer, feeling the heat radiate between us.

It's dangerous, and it's wrong, but right now, I don't care.

All I want is him.

He's already hard as hell, and I can't resist—I reach for him, feeling his length straining against the fabric. This time, I'm more confident. I'm not a virgin anymore, and I know exactly what he's capable of. He knows how to take good care of me.

Feeling bold, I slip his cock out of his shorts and start stroking it bare, loving the way he growls in response. His cock is thick and hot in my hand, pulsing with need as I wrap my fingers around it and give it a slow, deliberate squeeze. I run my thumb over the tip, smearing the bead of pre-cum that's already forming there, and I can't help but smile at how responsive he is.

I work my hand up and down his length, loving the way he feels—so solid and ready, each stroke drawing another low, sensual growl from him. Part of me wonders if I could make him explode just like this, with nothing but my hand..

Before I can find out, he pulls back slightly, his eyes dark with intent. "I want to taste you," he growls, his voice thick with desire.."

Before I can respond, he scoops me up like I weigh nothing at all, carrying me over to one of the benches. He sets me down gently, his strong hands guiding me as if I'm something precious. I'm totally exhilarated, my heart racing as I anticipate what's coming next.

He kisses me deeply, his lips demanding and hot against mine. "I've been fantasizing about peeling you out of these yoga clothes," he murmurs, his voice sending a shiver down my spine.

He peels off my top, and my breasts spill out, free from the confines of my sports bra. He doesn't hesitate, his mouth immediately finding my nipples, kissing and sucking them until I'm practically squirming beneath him. The heat from his mouth travels down my body as he kisses my stomach, slowly pulling down my leggings to reveal the black thong I'd almost forgotten I was wearing.

Every nerve in my body is on fire, and I feel like I'm going to explode.

He kisses my thighs, his lips brushing over my skin like he's worshiping every inch of me. Each kiss sends a jolt of pleasure through me, making me tremble with anticipation. When he finally pulls down my thong, I'm already soaked, desperate for him to touch me where I need it most.

His mouth is on me instantly, devouring me with a hunger that makes my head spin. His tongue moves in perfect rhythm, licking and swirling over my clit with just the right amount of pressure. And then his fingers join in, sliding into me, curling just right to hit the spot inside that drives me wild.

The combination is insane. His tongue flicks and teases my clit while his fingers pump in and out of my impossibly slick pussy, each thrust perfectly timed to push me closer to the edge. He's relentless, the pleasure building and building until it's almost too much to bear. I'm writhing on the bench, gripping the edges like it's the only thing keeping me grounded.

He pauses just long enough to look up at me, his eyes dark with desire. "You taste fucking amazing," he growls, his voice full of raw, animalistic hunger.

Through the haze of pleasure, it hits me just how good he makes me feel about my body, about every inch of me.

He doubles down, his tongue and fingers working in perfect harmony, and I can't hold back. The orgasm crashes over me, hard and fast, making me cry out as my pussy clenches around his fingers. I come so hard, it leaves me breathless, my mind a blur of pure, unfiltered ecstasy.

He stands up, licking my juices off his lips, that cocky grin on his face as he looks down at me.

I rise to my feet, feeling a rush of confidence. I pull off his sleeveless shirt, my hands roaming over his gorgeous upper body—those chiseled pecs, rock-hard abs, and the way his muscles tense under my touch. I can't resist him, can't resist leaning in to kiss his chest, trailing my lips down to his abs.

Is this how he feels about me? Like an animal, unable to get enough?

He takes off the rest of his clothes, standing there completely naked, and grins at me. I narrow my eyes playfully. "Why are you grinning like that?"

Without a word he guides me to the weight bench, that mischievous grin never leaving his face. I lie back, my heart racing in anticipation, spreading my legs as he positions himself between them. The cool leather of the bench presses against my skin, grounding me as I prepare for what's coming next.

He stands there for a moment, looking down at me like I'm a feast laid out just for him. His cock, hard and ready, is the perfect contrast to the dark intensity in his eyes. He leans in, his hands sliding down my thighs before gripping my hips, pulling me closer to the edge of the bench.

"You ready for this?" he growls, his voice thick with desire.

"More than ready," I whisper, my hands gripping the sides of the bench for leverage.

He thrusts into me, deep and powerful. The angle is perfect, the bench giving him all the support he needs to drive into me with relentless force. I can feel every inch of him filling me completely, and it's everything I didn't know I needed.

"Fuck, you feel so good," he groans, his hands guiding my movements, pushing me to meet every thrust. "You like this, don't you? Being taken right here, like this?"

"Yes," I gasp, the pleasure overwhelming as he pounds into me, each thrust hitting just right. "Don't stop."

"I'm not stopping until you come for me."

He keeps going, his pace unrelenting, driving me closer and closer to the edge. The bench creaks beneath us, but I'm too lost in the sensation to care. It doesn't take long before the pleasure builds to an unbearable peak, and I'm crying out his name as I come hard, my body trembling with the force of it.

After catching our breath, Nico's eyes flick to the squat rack, and I can almost see the wheels turning in his head. He grins, a devilish, commanding grin that makes my knees weak.

"We're not done yet," he says, grabbing my hand and pulling me toward the squat rack. My heart races as I realize what he has in mind, and a thrill of excitement rushes through me.

He adjusts the bar to the perfect height, then guides me to bend over it, my hands gripping the cool metal for support. I'm fully exposed, my body tingling with anticipation as he positions himself behind me. I can feel his cock, still rock hard, pressing against me, and I know this is going to be intense.

He slides into me, filling me completely. The angle is perfect, the bar giving me the leverage I need to push back against him with each powerful thrust. The mirrored wall in front of us shows every movement, every thrust, and I can't tear my eyes away from the sight of him fucking me like this.

"Look at yourself," he commands, his voice low and rough as he pounds into me. "Watch how good you look getting fucked by me."

I do as he says, my eyes locked on our reflection. The sight of him behind me, his muscles flexing as he drives into me, sends a new wave of pleasure coursing through me. The combination of his deep thrusts and the way he's talking to me is too much, and I feel the tension building fast.

"I'm gonna come," I gasp, my voice shaky with the intensity of watching our reflection.

"Do it," he growls, his pace quickening. "Come for me. Come all over my cock. I want to feel it."

The orgasm hits me like a tidal wave, my body trembling as I clench around him. Right at the peak, he lets go, coming hard inside me, filling me with his heat.

The sensation is overwhelming, the pleasure so intense I can hardly breathe, and I can feel every pulse of his release as it drives me over the edge again.

We slow down, both of us catching our breath. I glance in the mirror one last time, taking in the sight of him behind me, glistening and gorgeous.

God, he looks like something out of a dream, all rugged and sweaty. When he finally slides out of me, I feel an immediate, almost desperate sense of loss. What the hell is going on with me? How do I feel so attached to this man already?

My eyes flash as I suddenly remember overhearing some jackass back in college bragging to his buddies about how he'd never want to be a virgin's first—said they get way too clingy. A wave of panic washes over me. Is that what's happening here? Is this some sort of chemical reaction I have no control over, making me feel things I shouldn't?

But as quickly as the panic comes, it melts away the moment he wraps his arm around me, guiding me gently to the floor. His touch is warm, reassuring, and as he pulls me close, I can't help the big, goofy smile that spreads across my face..

I feel safe, content, and maybe even a little smitten. Lying here in his arms, the rest of the world seems to disappear..

Maybe it's just the afterglow, or maybe it's something more, but right now, I don't care.

CHAPTER 11

NICO

We're lying there in a comfortable silence, the kind that comes after you've just shared something intense.

But outOut of nowhere, Willow sits up. I watch as she turns to me with a worried expression, her eyes flicking over my face like she's searching for something. She doesn't say a word, and it starts to gnaw at me.

"What?" I ask, my voice steady, though I can sense there's something serious on her mind. She hesitates, biting her lip in that way she does when she's unsure of herself. I don't like seeing her uncertain, so I gently push her, trying to get her to open up. "Come on, Willow. Out with it."

Finally, she takes a breath and asks, "Is this what you hired me for?"

I'm confused, not quite following her. "This?" I repeat, raising an eyebrow.

"Yeah. You know. *This*." She gestures around us, her meaning sinking in a second later.

Sex.

A flicker of offense runs through me. I sit up, leveling her with a steady look. "First off, Ms. M hired you. I had no hand in the selection process beyond giving final approval—and I hadn't even seen what you looked like before then." My tone is firm, but I want her to understand there's no hidden agenda here. "You were brought on because you were the right fit for my girls, not for anything else."

I see the tension in her ease slightly, but there's still a shadow of doubt in her eyes, one I'll need to address. And I can tell there's more she's not saying.

She gets up, moving toward her clothes, picking them up one by one. I watch her as she pulls on her thong and then her sports bra, her movements deliberate but graceful.

"You said the other night this would never happen again."

I shake my head. "I know. But dammit Willow, there's just something about you."

She nods and looks down. "I know. I feel it too. I told myself I wouldn't get caught up again."

"Me either, but here we are. I have to warn you though, this can be a physical thing only," I clarify, watching her reaction closely.

She narrows her eyes, not in anger, but in sharp, calculated thought, processing my words.

I keep going, knowing it's better to be up front. "I know this sounds callous, but I don't want you getting any ideas about a relationship starting between us. I don't have the time or inclination for it."

I see her absorb what I've said, her expression unreadable. I know it's a lot to lay out like this, but it's better she knows where I stand. I can't afford complications, no matter how much I'm drawn to her. She needs to understand that clearly.

"This is about keeping things simple," I say.

She stays quiet at first, slipping into her leggings with a practiced ease. I take one last hungry glance at her perfect ass before it disappears underneath the fabric with a satisfying snap.

As she pulls on her tank top, I wonder if I've pushed her too far. Maybe she feels rejected, or worse, humiliated.

She checks the iPad, her face giving nothing away. I quickly get dressed too, pulling on my shorts and shirt, all the while keeping an eye on her, trying to read her. The silence stretches on, making me wonder if I've screwed this up.

Finally, she turns to me, her eyes locking onto mine with a steady, unflinching gaze.. "I'm not looking to get attached to you either."

The relief that floods through me is immediate, though I don't let it show. Instead, I give her a slow nod, acknowledging her words. There's a confidence in her tone, in the way she carries herself now, that wasn't there before. It's like she's made her decision and is sticking to it, no hesitation.

"Good," I say, my voice equally firm.. "That's exactly what I wanted to hear."

She turns back to the iPad, her attention shifting, and I can't help but admire the way she handled that. She knows what she wants, and I respect that. This is exactly how it needs to be—simple, just like we agreed.

I continue, making sure there's no room for misunderstanding. "Just because we're adding this extra dimension to our relationship doesn't mean I don't expect you to stay on top of your nanny duties."

She snaps her head up, flashing me a hard look that's all fire. "I would never neglect the girls, and I sure as hell wouldn't use my body to get out of doing my job."

I let out a low chuckle. "Seems like I offend you pretty easily."

She rolls her eyes but can't hide the smile tugging at her lips. "Yeah, well, maybe you should work on your delivery."

Her laughter fills the room, a sound I find myself enjoying more than I expected. There's something about it that lightens the air, easing the tension I didn't even realize I was holding onto.

I give her a small nod, still smirking. "Alright, Willow. Go enjoy your day off."

She nods, gathering her things and heading toward the door.

This arrangement might be unconventional, but I'm confident it's the right move for both of us.

Simple, straightforward, and no strings attached—just the way I like it.

CHAPTER 12

NICO

I watch Willow leave, the sway of her hips drawing my eyes until she throws a smile over her shoulder just before stepping out of the gym. The second she's out of sight, a pang of regret hits me, a part of me wishing she'd come back.

Shaking it off, I step onto the treadmill, determined to get in a solid run and clear my mind. I pick up the pace, the familiar rhythm of my feet hitting the belt usually a good way to focus. But today, it's different. My legs feel a little heavier than usual, and it doesn't take long to realize why—I'm already a bit worn out from the workout I just had with Willow.

A grin tugs at my lips as I slow the treadmill down. The memory of her under me, the way she moaned my name, it's all still too fresh, too vivid. The run can wait—it seems I've already gotten my heart rate up plenty this morning.

I step off the treadmill, wiping the sweat from my brow. Instead of pushing through a workout I don't really need, I head straight for the shower. The hot water's going to feel damn good, and maybe it'll help clear my head, get me back to the business I should be focusing on.

But as I strip down and step under the spray, I know it's not going to be that easy to shake Willow from my mind.

I let the hot water rush over me, savoring the last traces of her scent on my skin before it's washed away. The warmth soothes my muscles, but it does nothing to ease the tension building inside me. The memory of Willow, bent over the squat rack, flashes in my mind, and I feel myself getting hard all over again.

I consider taking care of it in the shower, just to clear my head. But I know better. That wouldn't be enough to erase the images of her, the way she felt, the way she fluttered around me. Those memories are going to be with me for a long, long time.

I shake my head, realizing this is already more than I bargained for. She's not just another woman; she's already making this more complicated than I intended. I wanted to keep things simple, strictly physical, but I can sense it—she's starting to get under my skin. And that could be dangerous.

I turn off the shower and grab a towel, drying off as I wrestle with the truth that's been gnawing at me. Maybe I'm getting in over my head with Willow. She's not just a fling to scratch an itch; there's something about her that's different, something that's already making me want more than I should.f

Wrapping the towel around my waist, I step out of the bathroom, ready to start the day. But no matter how hard I try to push her out of my mind, she's there, lingering in the back of my thoughts.

I get dressed in my room and head downstairs just in time to see my little girls bursting through the door with Ms. M, fresh from their trip to the park. The moment they spot me, their faces light up, and they rush toward me with such enthusiasm their hugs nearly knock me off my feet.

"Papa!" Giulia squeals, clinging to my leg, while Lucia wraps her arms around my waist, looking up at me with those big, innocent eyes.

"Do you still have to do work, Papa?" Lucia asks, her voice tinged with hopeful curiosity I can never resist.

Readjusting my priorities, I shake my head. "Not a chance," I say, ruffling her hair. "I'm going to spend the rest of the day with my little princesses like I promised." Their squeals of delight fill the room, and it's impossible not to feel the warmth of their joy. "How about we make it a special day? What do you say we go to the zoo?"

Their eyes widen with excitement, and they both start bouncing on their toes, practically bursting with happiness. "Yes! Yes!" they chant, almost in unison.

I turn to Ms. M, who's watching the scene with a soft smile. "Take the day for yourself, Ms. M. We've got it from here."

"You got it. I'll be around if you need anything," she replies.

"Did they have breakfast yet?" I ask, noticing how hungry I'm starting to feel myself.

"Just a little fruit and yogurt to start," she says.

"Well then," I grin, turning to the girls. "How about some of Papa's famous chocolate French toast before we head out?"

Their eyes go wide, and they both nod enthusiastically. "Yes, please!" they shout, and I laugh at their infectious excitement.

We head into the kitchen, the girls chattering excitedly as I gather the ingredients for our breakfast.

"Papa, can I stir?" Giulia asks, standing on her tiptoes to peek into the bowl.

"Of course, princess," I say, handing her the whisk. "Just like this—nice and steady."

Lucia, not wanting to be left out, tugs on my shirt. "I want to dip the bread!"

"Alright, alright, one at a time," I chuckle, guiding her over to the bread. "You dip it in the egg mix, just like this, and make sure it's all covered."

Soon, the kitchen is filled with the sweet smell of cooking French toast, and the girls are grinning from ear to ear as we work together. Once the toast is golden brown and drizzled with chocolate, they're sitting down at the table, practically bouncing with excitement.

Just as I think Willow must have left, she swings through the kitchen, catching me by surprise. "Just wanted to say goodbye to my little ladies," she says, a warm smile on her face.

"We're having Papa's chocolate French toast, and we're going to the zoo!" Lucia announces, beaming.

Willow smiles. "Sounds like a perfect day. Have so much fun, and I'll see you this evening."

Before she can leave, the girls rush over to hug her, holding her tight. "Come with us!" they plead; their voices full of innocent insistence.

I watch as the girls go absolutely crazy over Willow, clinging to her like she's their favorite person in the world. It's captivating, the way she's so at ease with them, her laughter mixing with theirs as they chat. Even though it's her day off, she's in no rush to leave, clearly enjoying the moment just as much as they are.

"*Please*, Willow, come with us!" Giulia begs, her arms wrapped tightly around Willow's waist.

"Yeah, we want you to see the lions and the monkeys!" Lucia adds, squeezing her legs.

Willow crouches down to their level, smiling warmly. "You know I'd love to, but today's your special day with your papa. Besides, I'll be here when you get back, and you can tell me all about the animals you saw. Deal?"

"Deal!" they both chirp, though they still don't let go of her..

I step in, gently helping Willow disentangle herself from their enthusiastic hugs. "Alright, girls, let Willow go. Your French toast is getting cold."

With some reluctance, they finally release her and scamper back to the table, digging into their breakfast. with gusto. I turn to Willow, noting the way the sunlight catches her hair, the playful glint in her eyes.

"What have you got planned for the day?" I ask, my voice casual, though there's a tension in the air that's hard to ignore.

She shrugs, tucking a strand of hair behind her ear. "I'm not sure yet. I thought I'd start with a walk around the neighborhood and take it from there."

Our eyes meet, and for a moment, the room feels charged with something unspoken. The air between us is thick with that same heated tension from earlier, and I can tell she feels it too. But instead of acting on it,

I nod. "Enjoy your walk."

She gives me a small smile , her gaze lingering on mine for a beat longer than necessary before she finally turns to leave.

The girls finish their breakfast, their plates nearly licked clean. "Alright, my little princesses," I say, clapping my hands to get their attention, "I need your help cleaning up."

They dive right into it, each one eager to impress. Giulia grabs her plate and hurries over to the sink, while Lucia carefully carries the syrup-sticky forks. They're quick and efficient, clearly enjoying the responsibility, and I can't help but smile at their enthusiasm.

As I'm wiping down the table, I catch a glimpse of Willow through the kitchen window. She's walking down the sidewalk in front of the house, her figure slowly disappearing as she heads off for her day.

A strange longing hits me square in the gut, an unexpected ache that's hard to shake.

It's her day off, and she's just the hired help, but the thought of spending the day without her almost makes it feel incomplete.

I push the feeling aside, telling myself she deserves her time to relax. But a part of me wishes she were joining us, seeing the girls' excitement firsthand, sharing in their laughter. We finish cleaning quickly and rush off to grab their coats, their excitement for the zoo practically bursting at the seams.

As they chatter about what animals they want to see, I find my thoughts still drifting back to Willow. I wonder if I've bitten off more than I can chew. This arrangement with her was supposed to be simple, physical—but nothing about how I feel right now is simple.

And it's definitely not just physical.

CHAPTER 13

WILLOW

"How many times have you come already?" Nico's voice comes out in a sexy growl, his breath hot against my neck.

I bite my lip, pretending to think. "Lost count," I pant.

I'm seated on his dresser, my thighs wrapped tight around his waist, and I'm gripping the edge for dear life. The wood creaks under us, but I couldn't care less. Each thrust sends a shockwave through me, pleasure radiating out like he's setting me on fire.

He flashes the wicked grin that makes me melt every damn time. "Get ready for one more."

I brace myself as he slams into me, deep and relentless, hitting that sweet spot over and over while his thumb traces circles over my clit. The pressure builds, coiling tight in my core, threatening to snap any second. But he holds me right on the edge, the bastard, dragging it out like he always does.

"Nico," I gasp, digging my nails into his shoulders. "Stop teasing me. You know what that does to me."

He chuckles, his breath ragged. "Can't help it. You're so fucking sexy when you're about to come."

"Selfish," I manage to tease back, even though I'm practically begging for release at this point.

His grip on my hips tightens, and he leans in close, his lips brushing mine. "Yeah, but you love it."

And damn it, he's right.

I glance down and watch as Nico's cock disappears deep into my pussy, over and over, each thrust making my breath hitch. It's hypnotic, the way his body moves with such raw intensity, every muscle working to drive me completely insane.

I feel his mouth latch onto my breast, his tongue flicking over my nipple as he sucks hard. The pleasure rockets through me, sharp and electric, dragging me right to the brink of release.

"Nico, I'm gonna come," I moan, my voice trembling with need.

He pulls back just enough to smirk at me, that cocky glint in his eyes. "Ask nicely, and I'll let you. And what's with this *Nico* talk? I'm your boss, remember?"

I roll my eyes, biting back a grin. "You're impossible, you know that?"

He raises an eyebrow, stilling his movements slightly. "That doesn't sound like asking nicely."

I huff, knowing exactly where this is going, but I play along. "Please, *Mr. Conti*, let me come."

He leans in, his voice a low rumble. "Beg."

I'm too far gone to argue. I let out a needy whine, arching into him. "Please. Please let me come. I need it. I need you."

His lips curve into a satisfied grin. "Good girl."

And then he's pounding into me again, harder, faster, taking me right over the edge. The orgasm rips through me, my whole body shaking with the force of it, and Nico's right there with me, groaning as he spills inside me. The feeling of him pulsing, filling me, sends one last wave of pleasure crashing over me. It's so damn good, I can't stop the shivers that rack my body as his cum spills down the inside of my thigh.

I collapse against Nico, panting as I try to catch my breath. His big arms wrap around me, holding me tight, and I melt into his warmth. The sex is mind-blowing, like always, but honestly, there's something almost better about the way he holds me after. His body is all hard muscle and heat, a safe haven I could stay in forever.

We stay like this for a bit, his cock still buried inside me, and I savor every second of it. Eventually, he slides out, and I can't help the little pang of loss that hits me. I always miss that connection the moment it's gone.

He heads over to the nightstand, and I can't take my eyes off him. The moonlight streaming in through the window paints his body in silver, highlighting every delicious line of muscle. And that ass? Damn, it's almost unfair how perfect it is—tight, firm, and just begging to be smacked.

He picks up the iPad monitor and glances at it, then turns to me with a smirk. "The girls are still asleep, if you're wondering."

"Good," I say. , half-joking, half-serious. "With the way you were screwing me, I was worried I was going to wake up the entire Upper West Side."

He flashes a cocky grin over his shoulder, the one that makes my heart do a little flip. "You probably almost did. But can you blame me? You're impossible to resist."

I get up, sauntering over to him with a sway in my hips. He turns toward me, his eyes shamelessly tracing over my curves, drinking me in like he's never seen me before. God, I love when he looks at me like that—hungry, eager, like he's ready to devour me all over again.

I wrap my arms around his shoulders, standing on my tiptoes to press my lips to his. He meets me halfway, his kiss playful, teasing me with just a flick of his tongue. I grin against his mouth, then playfully tug him back toward the bed. We tumble onto the sheets, and I curl up next to him, my head resting on his chest.

He raises an eyebrow, smirking. "What, you want another go-around already?"

"Nah," I reply, snuggling closer. "I just want to lie here with you like this."

He obliges, wrapping his big arm around me, pulling me in tight. I sigh, letting myself enjoy the quiet moment, his heartbeat steady under my ear. But there's something on my mind, something I can't help but ask.

"Can I ask you a question?"

He tenses slightly, and I can see a flicker of apprehension in his eyes, but he nods. "Go for it."

I take a deep breath, not sure how he'll react. "Do you ever wish we could sleep in bed together?"

His expression shifts, the playful teasing gone, replaced with something much more serious. He looks at me, really looks at me, like he's weighing his words carefully.

Then Nico sighs, running a hand through his hair like he's gearing up for a lecture. "We agreed from the beginning that this was just physical. And don't forget the girls—what if they walked in and saw us lying in bed together? Imagine how confused they'd be."

I bite my lip, feeling like I just stepped into territory I'm not supposed to, but I can't back down now. Something inside me needs to push this.

"Okay, okay, chill. I get it. But let's say, hypothetically, this is just a thought experiment. If there were no consequences —like, none—would you want that?"

He gives me a look, like he's trying to figure out if I'm for real right now. "Willow, there are *always* consequences."

I open my mouth to argue, but then I stop. I can tell this isn't going anywhere. He's got that wall up, the one I'm never going to break through. I let out a long sigh, feeling the frustration build up, but I don't push it further.

"Are you still fine with this no-strings-attached arrangement?" he asks, his tone casual, but I can hear the edge underneath.

"Yeah, totally," I say quickly, forcing a smile. But deep down, something shifts, and I'm not so sure anymore. .

The words taste like a lie, and I hate that. Because if I'm being honest with myself, I think maybe I want more than just the hookup. Maybe I'm starting to catch feelings, and that's a whole mess I'm not ready to deal with.

I slide off the bed, stretching my arms above my head. "I should probably head back to my room," I say, trying to keep my tone light.."

Nico nods, agreeing. "Yeah, probably for the best."

I step into my panties and pull on my oversized T-shirt, the fabric soft against my skin. Just as I'm about to head for the door, Nico rises and strides over to me. My eyes flick down, catching sight of his manhood, still heavy and long, hanging between his muscular thighs.

He puts his hands on my hips and pulls me close, his touch sending a shiver up my spine. "I'm still really enjoying this, you know. But if you're not..."

I cut him off, flashing a quick smile. "No, I am. For real."

He leans in, kissing me slow and deep, the kind of kiss that makes my knees weak and my brain forget all the reasons I should be keeping my distance. It's the kind of kiss that makes me think I'd put up with anything just to be close to him like this.

When he finally pulls away, he gives me a playful swat on the ass, and I can't help but giggle. "See you in the morn-ing," he says, his voice low and warm.

"What are you in the mood for, breakfast-wise?"

He grins, that cocky smile I can't get enough of. "Surprise me."

I slip out of his room, my heart doing a weird little dance in my chest as I head back to mine.

I make my way down the hallway, tiptoeing like I'm sneaking out after curfew. Already, I miss Nico's warmth, the way he makes me feel all melty inside. It's kind of pathetic, honestly, but I can't help it.

When I slip into my room and shut the door behind me, my mind starts racing. It's been three weeks since this whole thing started, and somehow, Nico and I have managed to fuck in just about every room in this damn house. And the wild part? I crave him more every day, like I'm addicted or something.

Honestly, it's low-key terrifying.

I've been poking at him, trying to get a read on where his head's at, if maybe he wants more than just the physical. But every time, he throws up this massive stone wall. He's got that whole emotionally unavailable vibe down to a science. It's maddening, and I'm not even sure what I'm hoping for. Do I really want more? Or am I just getting too caught up in all this?

I flop down on the bed, staring up at the ceiling, my thoughts swirling around. I'm almost a month into this gig, and I can't help but wonder—what's month two going to look like? More of the same? Or is something going to change?

Before I can dive too deep into that mess, a wave of nausea hits me out of nowhere, making my stomach churn. What the hell?

I bolt to the bathroom, dropping to my knees just in time to hurl everything in my stomach.

This isn't the first time I've felt queasy out of nowhere this week, but it's the first time I've actually thrown up. I sit back on my heels, wiping my mouth with the back of my hand, trying to figure out what's going on.

Tomorrow's Monday, and thankfully, I've got the afternoon off. Ms. M's taking the twins to the pediatrician for their checkup after preschool, so maybe I can squeeze in a visit to my own doctor – after my lunch date with Kendall, of course.

Last thing I need is to be too sick to work. I can't let anything mess up this job—Nico or no Nico.

I take a deep breath, trying to steady myself as I get up from the floor. Whatever this is, I just need to handle it. I glance in the mirror, my reflection looking a little more pale and tired than usual. I shake it off, deciding that tomorrow, I'm going to get to the bottom of whatever's going on.

CHAPTER 14

WILLOW

I wake up the next morning feeling like I've been hit by a damn truck. Before I even have a chance to fully open my eyes, a nasty wave of nausea hits me, slamming into me hard. I bolt to the bathroom, barely making it before I'm hunched over the toilet, throwing up again.

This time, it's all dry heaves, and it's brutal. My whole body feels like it's been wrung out and left to dry.

When it's finally over, I sit back on the cold tile floor, gasping for breath. What the hell is going on with me? This feels like the hangover from hell, except I haven't touched a drop of booze.

I drag myself up and over to the sink, splashing cold water on my face and trying to shake off the grossness. As I look at my reflection, something feels... off. I can't put my finger on it, but there's definitely something different staring back at me.

Then, out of nowhere, a thought hits me like a ton of bricks.

What if I'm pregnant?

The idea sends a cold spike of fear straight through my gut. My stomach clenches, and I grip the edge of the sink, feeling like the floor just dropped out from under me. I mean, it's possible, right? Nico and I have been going at it like rabbits, and sure, I'm on the pill, but nothing's 100%.

Oh, shit. What if I'm actually pregnant?

My mind's racing as I think back, trying to remember if I've been as religious with the pill as I should've been. With everything going on—this job, the fling with Nico—it's all been such a blur. I reach into my drawer and pull out my pill case, flipping it open with shaky hands. And sure enough, there it is, staring me right in the face: two pills I straight-up forgot to take, just chilling there like a couple of traitors. I was so wrapped up in everything I didn't even notice.

I groan, running a hand through my hair. This is exactly the kind of stupid mistake I never thought I'd make. But here we are, and now I've got to deal with the consequences— whatever they might be.

Just then, my alarm goes off, jolting me out of my spiraling thoughts. Time to get the girls up and start the day. I shake off the panic, forcing myself to focus. There's nothing I can do about this right now, so I need to keep it together until I can get to the pharmacy later. I rinse out my mouth, brushing my teeth like I can scrub away the anxiety, and then quickly get dressed.

As I pull on my clothes, I make a silent vow to stay cool, keep my head in the game. I've got a job to do, and freaking out isn't going to help anything. Once I've handled my work, then I'll figure out what the hell to do next.

I head to the girls' room to get them ready for preschool, but to my surprise, they're already up and giggling, playing with their toys. "Well, look at you two," I say with a grin. "Got you so well-trained, you don't even need me to wake you up!"

"Morning, Willow!" Lucia says, an adorable grin on her face.

"Morning!" Giulia adds.

I make a mental note to stay focused today, not let my possible baby drama mess with my head. The girls deserve my full attention, and I'm not about to slack off because my brain's doing cartwheels.

I help them into their clothes, keeping the morning routine smooth and easy, and we head downstairs together. For once, I'm actually relieved that Nico isn't around. He's the absolute last person I want to see right now. I need space to think.

As we reach the bottom of the stairs, I freeze. My blood runs cold at the sound of a deep, resonant voice coming from the kitchen.

"Papa!" the girls scream, tearing away from me and sprinting into the kitchen.

I follow them, my heart pounding in my chest. And there he is, casually chatting with Ms. M like it's just another morning. My stomach flips as I watch him, trying to keep my cool even though I'm freaking out on the inside..

I take a deep breath, trying to steady my nerves, and step into the kitchen. The girls are already wrapped around Nico's legs, their little faces beaming up at him.

"Papa, Papa! Guess what? We woke up all by ourselves today!" Giulia chirps.

"Yeah, we're big girls now!" Lucia adds, giggling.

Nico crouches down, ruffling their hair with a warm smile. "Well, look at that! My big girls are growing up so fast. You're making Papa proud."

Seeing Nico with the girls is always adorable, but today, it hits different. My mind starts spinning as I realize that I could be pregnant with a new little brother or sister for the girls, a new daughter or son for Nico. He's such a loving dad, but the thought of telling him I might be carrying his child? That's a whole other level of anxiety.

"Morning," I say, trying to sound as normal as possible as I greet Nico and Ms. M.

"Morning, Willow," Ms. M replies with a smile.

I steal a glance at Nico. His sleeves are rolled up, showing off his taut forearms. I watch the way his Adam's apple bobs as he sips his coffee, and damn it, why does he have to be so effortlessly hot?

He catches me looking, and a sly grin spreads across his face, like he knows exactly what's on my mind. I look away too quickly.

Nico glances at his fancy-ass watch, the kind that probably costs more than my entire wardrobe. "I've got to get moving," he says, sounding all businesslike. But then he pauses, his brow furrowing for a moment as if he's just remembered something. "Wait, today's the girls' pediatrician appointment, right?"

The girls groan in unison, clearly not thrilled about it.

Ms. M steps in with her usual calm. "Come on, now. Dr. Rodriguez is very nice, and she's just going to make sure you're in tip-top shape. It won't take long."

The girls give in, though not without a bit of pouting.

Nico turns to Ms. M. "You're taking them?"

Ms. M nods. "It's easier with the paperwork and everything if I handle it. I can pick them up after lunch at school."

Nico gives a small nod of approval. "Makes sense. Willow, we talked about you taking the afternoon off, correct?"

I smile and nod. He's all business now, clearly shifting into work mode. He gives the girls a quick kiss on the head and a nod to Ms. M and me before heading out the door.

As soon as he's gone, my phone buzzes in my pocket. It's a text from Kendall, my cousin: *Can't wait to catch up later! Coffee's on me!*

It's later in the day, and Ms. M just left to get the girls. They won't be back until dinner, so I've got a solid four hours of me-time. First up, coffee with Kendall.

Part of me is tempted to take the pregnancy test before heading out, but honestly, I need a break from my own brain. Kendall's the perfect person to help me chill; she's always had a way of making everything feel a little less serious.

I throw on a coat and step out into the crisp air. The sun's out, but there's still a bit of snow clinging to the ground, sparkling like it's trying to remind everyone that winter's just begun. I make my way to Bushwick, where Kendall lives, and head straight for our favorite coffee spot.

As soon as I walk in, I spot Kendall, her tall frame at the counter.

"Will!" she exclaims as soon as she sees me, rushing over to pull me into a tight hug.

"Kendall!" I hug her back, feeling some of the tension in my chest start to ease. She always knows how to make me feel at home, even when everything else is chaos..

"I'm so happy to see you!" she beams, squeezing me again before letting go.

"Same. It's been way too long," I reply, trying to match her energy even though my brain's still spinning..

"I'll grab us some coffee," she offers, heading back to the counter.

"Sure," I say, but then I freeze. Wait, aren't pregnant women supposed to avoid caffeine?

"Uh, actually," I call out, feeling super awkward, "can you get me something caffeine-free?"

Kendall turns and gives me a funny look. "Caffeine-free? You, Will? Since when?"

I scramble for an excuse, feeling like a total idiot. "Oh, uh, I've just been, you know, trying to cut back. Health kick or whatever."

She raises an eyebrow but doesn't push it. "Alright, how about a chai latte? It's still delicious and caffeine-free."

"Perfect," I say, trying to sound casual as I plop into a seat. As soon as I sit down, I realize I'm not off to a great start if I'm already fumbling to keep this whole thing under wraps. Kendall's no fool—she'll catch on if I'm not careful.

Kendall heads to the table with the drinks, talking a mile a minute like always. "So, how's the new job going? And those girls—oh my God, they're so cute in those pics you sent! And your boss—what's he like? Also, I've been thinking, we should totally do another joint yoga class soon. My students loved it last time! We could mix it up, maybe throw in some meditation or something? What do you think?"

She's a total yapper, but that's one of the things I love about her. When she's in full-on chatter mode, I don't have to worry about filling the silence. It's a blessing right now, especially with all the crazy thoughts bouncing around in my head.

Just as I'm about to answer, Kendall suddenly cocks her head to the side, eyes narrowing a little like she's picked up on something. "There's something different about you."

Oh shit. I try to play it cool, but my stomach does a nervous flip. "Different? Nah, just, you know, life stuff." I give a little laugh, hoping it doesn't sound as fake as it feels.

But Kendall's too sharp for her own good, and I can tell she's not buying it.

She squints, leaning in a little like she's trying to solve some big mystery. "I don't know... your skin, maybe? It looks, like, glowy or something. Are you using a new routine? You know, I just started this thing with niacinamide and hyaluronic acid—total game-changer. My pores? Practically invisible. And don't even get me started on the ceramide moisturizer—my skin has never felt so soft."

She's off on her skincare tangent, but I can barely focus. My heart's pounding, and I feel like I'm on the verge of cracking wide open. I can't keep it in anymore. The words are just sitting there, heavy on my tongue, waiting to spill out.

Kendall pauses, mid-rant, and tilts her head again, this time with genuine concern in her eyes. "Will... what's wrong?"

And just like that, I lose it. The dam breaks. "I think I might be pregnant."

Her eyes go wide, and for a second, everything's dead silent, like the world just hit pause.

"Wait, *what*?"

CHAPTER 15

WILLOW

Twenty minutes later, we're standing in the pregnancy test aisle at CVS, and Kendall's going through every single box like she's studying for an exam.

"Wow, they're all digital now," she says, flipping a box over to read the back.

I'm standing behind her, feeling totally disconnected from my body, like this isn't really happening.

Kendall notices, of course. She's been my rock since I blurted everything out back at the coffee shop. She comes over and puts a hand on my shoulder, giving it a reassuring squeeze. "It's gonna be okay, Will. No matter what, we've got this."

I nod, but I can barely find my voice to respond. My mind's spinning, a thousand thoughts racing through it, none of them sticking long enough to make any sense.

Kendall finally picks out a test she's confident about. "This one looks good," she says, then zips over to the freezer section like she's on a mission. She comes back with a pint of Cherry Garcia, our go-to whenever shit hits the fan. "Figured we could use this too."

Her hands full, she leads us to the register, her arm around my shoulders the whole way. I'm barely able to utter a word, but I'm grateful she's here. I don't know what I'd do without her right now.

My insides are in full-on panic mode. I check my phone—still got a couple of hours before I need to get back. Plenty of time to figure out if my whole life is about to change.

"Let's head over to my place," Kendall says, already steering us in that direction. "We can take the test there, assuming my roommates aren't hogging the bathroom."

We reach her building—a three-story walk-up that's seen better days—and I'm silently grateful none of her roommates are around. The place is small and kind of cramped, the typical Brooklyn apartment, and it hits me how lucky I am to be able to stay at Nico's spacious townhouse.

Kendall leads me straight to the bathroom, where we both just stand there for a second, staring at the pregnancy test box like it's some kind of alien artifact. Finally, she rips it open and holds up the test, her eyes meeting mine with a reassuring smile. "Alright, Will—do your thing."

I take the test from her, my hands shaking slightly. This is it. No turning back now.

Kendall gives me a reassuring squeeze on the arm before stepping back. "I'll give you some privacy. Gonna get the ice cream ready. Remember, whatever happens, you've got this."

I manage a small smile. "Thanks."

Then I thank her, appreciating how she's holding it together when I feel like I'm about to fall apart. I follow the directions and hold my breath for what feels like the whole two-minute wait. The timer on my phone goes off and I look down.

Positive.

I'm pregnant.

Holy. Freaking. Shit.

I stand there for a moment, staring at the word like it's written in a language I don't understand. Then, in a daze, I walk out of the bathroom, clutching the test in my hand. Kendall's in the kitchen, scooping the Cherry Garcia into two bowls. She looks up as I come in, concern flashing in her eyes.

"What does it say?" she asks, her voice gentle.

All I can do is nod, my throat too tight to speak.

Kendall's eyes widen, and she's by my side in an instant, pulling me into a hug. "Oh, Will."

And just like that, the reality of it all starts to sink in. The tears come out of nowhere, and before I can even say a word, I'm full-on ugly crying. Kendall guides me to the couch with that no-nonsense, big-sis energy she's so good at. She opens Spotify on her phone with a few quick swipes, connecting to her speaker system, the strains of *Lullaby* by Lorde drifting out.

She wraps her arms around me as we sit, letting me cry it out. After a few minutes, she asks softly, "What's going on in that head of yours? Are you crying because you're happy, or sad, or... what?"

I wipe my eyes, trying to pull myself together. "I don't know," I admit, taking a deep breath. Kendall hands me some tissues, and I blow my nose, feeling a little more like myself. "I think I'm happy. But I'm also scared."

"Scared about being pregnant?" she asks, concern written all over her face.

I hesitate, knowing I've got to spill the truth now.. "Not just that. I didn't tell you who the father is. Who I've been hooking up with."

She raises an eyebrow, immediately jumping to the worst conclusion. "Please don't tell me it's some random from Hinge or something."

I shake my head, but the truth is just as heavy. "No. It's my boss."

Kendall's jaw drops, and for a moment, she's completely speechless. I can see the wheels turning in her head, trying to process what I just dropped on her. This was not what she expected to hear. She blinks hard, shaking her head like she's trying to clear it. "You're serious? You've been screwing your boss?"

More tears well up in my eyes, and I sniffle. "Well, when you put it like that, it sounds so slutty."

Kendall's expression softens instantly. "No, no, that's not what I meant. I just—wow, Will. This is a lot." She pauses, curiosity lighting up her face. "So, this guy... he's rich, right?"

I nod, wiping my eyes. "Yeah."

"That's good," Kendall says, nodding like she's trying to find a silver lining. "Not that I'm a gold digger or anything, but, you know, at least he can take care of expenses and stuff."

"Or," I counter, "just cut me a check and send me on my way."

Kendall's eyes widen, and she's suddenly full of even more questions. "Wait, you were a virgin, right? Holy shit, that means you got pregnant by the first guy you slept with?"

I can't help but give a little laugh through the tears. "I know, right? Only me."

Kendall sighs, pulling me in for another hug. "Okay, we're going to figure this out. No matter what happens, we'll handle it. You're not alone in this, okay?" Then her eyes light up with curiosity. "Okay, spill. I need deets on this guy."

I roll my eyes and smile. "Well, he's older—like, definitely not in our age range. He's kind of a dick sometimes, but he's also sweet when he wants to be. And he really loves his little girls."

Kendall's expression softens. "A good dad? That's a great sign, Will. Shows he's got a heart." She grins, leaning in a little closer. "But l what about the sex?"

I gasp, playfully scandalized. "Kendall! Oh my God, you're such a perv."

She laughs, shrugging. "I'm just curious! Sorry, not sorry."

I purse my lips, trying to find the right words. "Well, he's very in control, you know? Like, he knows exactly what he's doing. And honestly? He practically worships my body. I mean, it's intense."

Kendall raises an eyebrow. "That sounds kinda hot."

I sigh, feeling the weight of it all. "Yeah, it is, but he's made it super clear that we're just a physical thing—nothing more serious. He's got these walls up, like, sky-high."

Kendall glances down at my belly, her grin fading slightly. "Well, whether he likes it or not, things just got pretty freaking serious."

"Yeah, no kidding."

Without missing a beat, she whips out her laptop, flipping it open with a determined look. "Alright, what's this guy's full name?"

"Nico Conti."

She starts typing and a few moments later, she pauses, her eyes narrowing at the screen. "Uh, Will... did you know he might be connected to the, uh, Conti Crime Family? As in, the Mob?"

I swallow hard, feeling my heart skip a beat. "Yeah, I did my research too. But he's never talked about it directly."

Kendall keeps scrolling, her expression serious. "Hold up. There's something else here. Looks like there was an article about the death of an Alessandro Conti. It says Nico's his son."

I blink, feeling a chill run down my spine. ""What does it say happened?"

"Looks like it was a Mob hit. Will, this is some serious stuff."

My stomach twists, the reality of everything sinking deeper than before.

Kendall keeps reading, her eyes scanning the screen with laser focus. "It says it was a suspected Mob hit at some restaurant in Astoria. Classic setup—broad daylight, no witnesses willing to talk. This is wild, Will."

With every word she reads, my nerves ratchet up another notch. My heart's pounding so hard I can barely hear anything else.

Kendall continues, "And get this—there's talk about Nico possibly taking over the entire Conti operation after his father's death. Some rumors even suggest he might've been the one to order the hit."

"No way," I blurt out, shaking my head in disbelief. "There's no way Nico's the type of guy who'd kill his own father." But as the words leave my mouth, I ask myself how well I really know this man.

Kendall gives me a serious look. "Will, this is huge. Like, world-altering huge. A guy like this..." She trails off, the implication hanging heavy between us.

I don't even know how to respond. My mind's spinning, trying to reconcile the man who's been so sweet and protective of his girls with the one I'm reading about in these articles. How could someone be both? And what the hell am I supposed to do now?

Kendall snaps her laptop shut, letting out a long breath. "Well, damn. This whole thing's taken more twists and turns than an episode of *Love Is Blind*. And I'm starting to get really worried that you're going to get wrapped up in all of this Mob nonsense."

I try to calm myself down, taking a deep breath. "Yeah, but Nico's good about keeping his family and his business separate. He doesn't mix that stuff. I've never seen him bring it home."

"It's great that he keeps his little girls out of it, but we both know it's impossible to say what might happen down the line. I mean, look at what happened to his dad."

I know she's right, and the thought just sits heavy in my chest. I can't predict what's coming, but it's clear this situation is more than just a casual fling gone complicated.

Kendall softens her tone. "Look, take this one day at a time, okay? But keep in the back of your head that you need to be ready for anything." Then, as if flipping a switch, she grins and stands up. "But you know what? We still gotta celebrate! You're going to be a mom! That's huge!"

She hops up and grabs the bowls of Cherry Garcia, bringing them over with a little wiggle in her step. We sit back down, and Kendall holds up her bowl. "To whatever the hell comes next!"

I can't help but laugh, clinking my bowl against hers.

"To whatever the hell comes next."

CHAPTER 16

Nico

"Alright girls," I say, "what's it going to be on the pizza tonight? No changing your minds once we decide."

I'm in the kitchen with Lucia and Giulia, both perched on the stools at the counter as we tackle the critical decision of pizza toppings. My laptop's open in front of us, and right now, nothing's more important than getting this right.

Lucia jumps in first. "Extra cheese!"

Giulia, not to be outdone, chimes in right after. "Pepperoni! And maybe mushrooms?"

I nod, considering their choices like they've just handed me a deal to close. "Extra cheese, pepperoni, and mushrooms. Good picks. But how about a supreme pizza? You know, with everything on it?"

They giggle, eyes wide as they think it over. Giulia suggests a compromise. "Maybe half and half?"

Smart move. "Half supreme, half pepperoni," I agree. "And we'll throw in an extra cheese pizza. Can't go wrong with that."

Ms. M walks by, grabbing a glass of water, and I glance her way. "You want anything, Ms. M?"

She smiles, lifting her glass. "Just a salad for me, thanks."

"Alright then, two pizzas it is. Extra cheese, half supreme, half pepperoni. And we'll add some breadsticks."

Lucia and Giulia cheer, clearly satisfied with the plan. But tonight isn't just about pizza. I've got something important in mind, and this dinner is only the beginning.

I pull out my phone and shoot Willow a quick text: *Are you on your way back?*

She replies almost immediately, saying she's on her way but got hung up in rush-hour train traffic. I fire a response to see if she's up for a pizza and movie night with the girls and me.

Sounds great, she texts back.

Good. That's exactly what I wanted to hear. I'm pleased, though I keep it to myself. I want to see how she fits into this dynamic, how she handles spending time with the girls and me like we're some kind of family. I'm not sure about making things more serious with her, but I'd be lying if I said the thought hasn't crossed my mind. A man doesn't ignore the possibility when it's staring him in the face.

With that settled, I head to the den with Lucia and Giulia. Disney+ is already fired up on the TV, so I hand the remote to them. "Alright, ladies, pick a movie."

They dive into a debate immediately—Lucia wants to watch *Moana* for the millionth time, while Giulia's pushing for *The Lion King*. Their back-and-forth is cute, both of them trying to convince the other with all the intensity of a high-stakes negotiation. I lean back, watching them with a half-smile.

Just as Lucia and Giulia settle on *The Lion King*, the door swings open and Willow walks in with the pizzas in hand. "Caught the delivery guy out front," she says with a grin, holding up the boxes like a trophy.

"Perfect timing," I reply, moving to grab plates and drinks from the kitchen. I set everything up on the coffee table and we all dig in, the scent of hot, cheesy pizza filling the room.

Willow immediately reaches for the supreme, and I watch, a bit surprised, as she starts putting it away with a vigor I didn't expect. She's usually more reserved, but tonight she's going for it like she hasn't eaten in days.

She notices me watching, and a flush creeps up her cheeks. "What? I'm hungrier than I thought," she says, half-apologetic, half-defiant.

I give her a small smile. "No need to explain. Just didn't realize you had such an appetite."

The girls are absolutely thrilled she's here. Lucia's practically bouncing in her seat, and Giulia keeps sneaking little smiles at Willow. It's clear they've warmed up to her, and the feeling seems mutual.

We settle in, plates in hand, as the movie starts. The room fills with the familiar sound of Disney magic, and I watch them out of the corner of my eye—my girls and Willow, all together. For a moment, everything feels right, like this is how it's supposed to be.

We're about halfway through the movie when the girls start clamoring for ice cream. I pause the movie and let them make their bowls, piling on toppings like there's no tomorrow. As they're busy, I turn to Willow. "How was your day?"

She takes a moment, as if considering how much to share. "It was good. Caught up with my cousin," she says, keeping it vague. She doesn't mention a name, and there's a slight hesitation in her voice that I don't miss.

I can tell there's something she's not telling me, something she's keeping under wraps. Part of me wants to press, to know what's going on in that head of hers. But I remind myself I don't have the right to know everything. We're not in that kind of relationship—at least, that's what I keep telling myself.

Still, the thought crosses my mind—did she meet up with some guy? The idea of her with someone else sends a sharp surge of jealousy through me, but I push it down. Not the time, and definitely not the place.

The girls return with their ice cream masterpieces, and we head back into the den. The movie picks up where we left off, and the room is filled with the sound of laughter and the occasional clink of spoons against bowls.

By the time the credits roll, both Lucia and Giulia are out cold, dozing peacefully against Willow. I watch them for a moment, feeling something deep in my chest tighten, but I shake it off. I scoop up Giulia while Willow gently gathers up Lucia, and we quietly carry them to bed.

Willow and I slip the girls into their pajamas, and as they wake up just a bit, she leans in to chat with them softly.

"Hey, sleepyheads," Willow says gently, brushing a stray hair from Lucia's face. "Did you have fun watching the movie?"

Lucia blinks sleepily and nods. "Yeah, it was good. Can we watch it again tomorrow?"

Giulia stirs, rubbing her eyes. "I want to watch *Moana* next time."

Willow chuckles softly. "Maybe we can have another movie night soon and watch both. How does that sound?"

The girls' eyes light up at the idea. "Yay!" they mumble, snuggling into their blankets.

I watch from the doorway, a smile tugging at my lips. When Willow finishes talking, I step over and gently kiss each of the girls on their foreheads. "Good night, my little princesses," I say. I make sure the monitor is in place, then slip out of the room with Willow.

The night has gone just as smoothly as I'd hoped.

As we head back to the living room, I turn to Willow and ask, "Got any plans for the rest of the evening?"

She gives me a small, playful smile. "Nope, just thinking about a bath and then bed."

I raise an eyebrow, grinning. "Want some company for that bath? Maybe you could use mine, since you seem so fond of it."

Willow bites her lower lip, her eyes sparkling with mischief.. "I'd like that."

The moment we step into the bedroom, my mind is racing with thoughts of what I'm going to do to Willow in that tub. The way she looks at me only adds fuel to the fire. But just as we're about to get started, my phone buzzes in my pocket.

I curse under my breath, holding up a finger to Willow. "I've got to take this. Go ahead and get the water going—I'll meet you in there."

She gives me a playful wink over her shoulder, pulling off her top as she disappears into the bathroom. The sight of her bare back as she vanishes into the bathroom makes it damn near impossible to focus on anything else.

I pull out my phone, expecting something trivial, but when I see Sal's name pop up, I know it's serious. The text is brief: *We need to meet tomorrow. Got some info on the hit—might be evidence linking it to a certain family we both know.*

A surge of fury rises in me, my fist clenching hard enough to make my knuckles white. The thought of the Rossis, and I know that's who he means, our longtime adversaries, murdering my father is infuriating.

I fire back a quick reply, telling Sal we'll meet tomorrow, then toss my phone onto the bed with more force than necessary. I need to deal with this, but not tonight.

Tonight, I have other plans, and nothing's going to ruin them.

Turning back toward the bathroom, I strip off my shirt, ready to join Willow and forget about the outside world for a while.

Willow is already in the tub, suds perfectly placed over her breasts in a way that drives me wild. I let my eyes roam over her body.

"Glad I get to join you in the tub this time," I say, my voice low and teasing, ". You know, instead of you sneaking in when I'm not around."

She laughs, a soft, musical sound that echoes off the tile.. "The universe must have a sense of humor, I guess."

I start toward her, every intention of sinking into that warm water and making her forget about anything outside this room. But something catches my eye—a glow from the counter. It's her phone, lighting up with a text. Instinctively, my gaze sharpens as IWithout thinking, I read the message on the screen: *Let's meet up again soon. Today was fun.*

The name attached to the text stops me cold—*Ken.*

"Ken?" I ask, my tone shifting, a sharp edge creeping in.

Willow's relaxed smile falters as she glances at her phone. I can see the gears turning in her head as she tries to figure out what to say.

I step to the edge of the tub, my hands on my hips, my eyes locked on hers. "Who's Ken?"

The jealousy roars inside me like a wildfire, but I keep it in check, reminding myself I was the one who set the rules. I was the one who said we were just having fun.

NANNY FOR THE DON | 123

It's not her fault that now I want more, especially so quickly.

"Are you seeing someone?"

She looks at me for a moment, and then, to my surprise, she laughs. The sound is light, almost teasing, and it catches me off guard.

"What's so funny?" I demand, my tone still sharp, but the edge is starting to soften.

"Get naked and get in the tub, and I'll tell you," she says, her eyes dancing with mischief.."

I narrow my eyes, not entirely convinced, but before I can say anything else, she playfully tosses a handful of bubbles at me, some landing on my chest.

I sigh, feeling the tension in the room ease just a bit. "Fine," I mutter, stripping off the rest of my clothes. ." I strip off my clothes and I slip into the warm water across from her, the heat instantly relaxing the muscles I hadn't realized were so tense.

Once I'm settled, she looks at me with a playful grin. "Ken is short for Kendall—my cousin. We've had this thing since we were kids where she calls me Will, and I call her Ken. Just something dumb we do."

I stare at her for a moment. , processing what she's said, and then I feel the tension leave my body completely. "Ken is Kendall," I repeat, a small smirk forming on my lips.

She nods., her eyes never leaving mine. "Now do you feel better, Mr. Suspicious?"

I lean back, the water lapping at my skin. "Yeah, I do."

She laughs again, a soft, teasing sound. "Sorry, but it was kind of funny how pissed you looked."

"I wasn't pissed," I reply , keeping my tone even as I lean back in the tub. "Just curious."

She gives me a knowing look, her grin widening. "*Suuure.*"

I don't bother elaborating, just lift an eyebrow in response, letting her think what she wants. But my mind drifts back to the look on her face when I mentioned Ken... almost like there's still something she's holding back. I push the thought aside for now, deciding it's a battle for another time.

"You know," she says. , her voice dropping to a playful whisper, "iIf I didn't know better, I'd swear you were getting a little possessive."

"It's not like that," I say, the words coming out a bit too quickly, even for my taste..

Her grin doesn't falter. "Look how tense you are." She scoots forward, closing the distance between us, and before I can react, she's sliding onto my lap. The warmth of her body against mine sends a jolt through me.

"Maybe," she murmurs, her lips brushing against my ear, "we need to do something to help you relax."

Her words are a challenge, one I'm more than ready to accept. My hands find her hips, gripping them with a possessiveness I won't admit to.

"Careful, *Will*," I warn, my voice low and controlled. "You might get more than you bargained for."

Her eyes flash with excitement. "Maybe that's exactly what I want."

Her fingers wrap around my cock, firm yet teasing, stroking me slowly as she looks up at me with those mischievous eyes. She leans in closer, her breath warm against my skin. "There's something I want to try," she says, her voice low and full of promise.

"What's that?" I ask, feeling the pleasure start to build.

"Sit on the edge of the tub," she commands, and something in her tone makes me want to obey without question. I shift, positioning myself on the cool edge, curiosity and arousal battling for control. The water drips off my skin, but all I can focus on is Willow as she moves between my legs.

She starts with my stomach, her lips brushing over my skin in a way that makes my muscles tighten. Each kiss is slow, deliberate, as she works her way down, taking her time to drive me wild. Her mouth moves lower, over my hips, across my thighs, until she's right where she wants to be.

When her lips touch my balls, I suck in a breath. Her tongue flicks out, testing, teasing, and I can feel the heat building inside me. She's got me right where she wants me, and she knows it.

Then she kisses along my shaft, slow and maddening, before taking me into her mouth. The feel of her lips sliding down over me, her tongue swirling around the tip—it's enough to make me lose all control.

She doesn't rush. She takes me in deeper, inch by inch, her mouth working me with a mix of softness and intensity that's almost too much to handle. I harden even more, completely at her mercy, and I fucking love it.

I watch Willow, completely transfixed. The sight of her so focused, so damn skilled, makes my blood sing. She's never done this before, not with anyone else, and that knowledge alone drives me crazy. I can feel the tension building, the orgasm starting to stir deep in the base of my cock.

Part of me wants to let go, to lose myself in the pleasure and watch her swallow every drop.

But I'm not ready to give in just yet.

Gritting my teeth, I gently guide her off me, even though every nerve in my body is screaming to let her finish. She looks up at me, a question in her eyes. "Was it good?" she asks, her voice a mix of uncertainty and mischief.

I can't help the smirk tugging at my lips. "Very good," I tell her, my voice rough with the effort it took to hold back. "But now it's my turn."

CHAPTER 17

WILLOW

His hands are all over me, sliding over my wet, soapy skin, teasing every inch of me.

He's got a wicked grin on his face, the one that makes my heart race and my body melt. His fingers find my nipples, pinching just enough to make me gasp, sending sparks of pleasure through me.

"You feel so good," he murmurs, his lips brushing against my ear. "I want to take you, make you mine right here."

He pulls me to my feet and bends me over the side of the tub, and I brace myself, breath hitching in anticipation.

Then I feel his tongue, warm and slick, finding its way to my slit. The first touch makes my legs tremble, my body arching toward him instinctively. He's teasing me, taking his time, and it's driving me wild. Every flick of his tongue, every soft caress, pushes me closer to the edge, making me forget everything except the feel of him, the way he's making me lose control as my juices drip down my thighs.

He's spread me open, and damn, his tongue is working wonders. I'm a moaning mess, so turned on I can barely think straight. Every swipe over my clit has me spiraling closer to the edge, and it's like he knows exactly how to play me, bringing me right to the brink before pulling back just enough to keep me craving more. It's maddening, this slow burn he's building.

"Fuck," I breathe out, my whole body tingling, desperate for release. And just when I think I can't take it anymore, he pushes me over the edge. The orgasm hits me like a wave, hard and fast, and I'm seeing stars. My mind goes blank, lost in the pure, dizzying pleasure he's wringing out of me.

Even as I'm coming down, he keeps talking, his voice low and dirty, like he's casting some kind of spell that leaves me totally bewitched.

I'm barely catching my breath when he moves, standing and positioning himself behind me. I can feel him pressing against me, hard and ready, and before I can even think, he's inside me, filling me up in one smooth glide.

"God, you feel so good," I gasp, my body trembling as he starts to move. He's thick and perfect, stretching me in just the right way, hitting every spot and making me want to scream.

It's like he's made to fit me, and every thrust is sending waves of pleasure through me, making me crave more and more.

He's fucking me slow and deep, each thrust making me lose my damn mind. He's got one hand in my hair, pulling just enough to send shivers down my spine, while the other hand smacks my ass, a sharp sting that somehow makes everything even hotter. I can't help but moan, biting my lip as the mix of pleasure and sting pushes me higher.

With a firm grip on my hair, he leans in close, his breath hot against my ear.

"You like that, don't you?" he growls, his voice low and dangerous. "You love being fucked like this, don't you, Willow? So wet, so tight, taking me so damn good. You were made for this; your tight little pussy was made for my cock."

His words send a fresh wave of heat through me, and I can't hold back the whimper that escapes. My body is on fire, every nerve ending tuned to him, desperate for more.

He knows exactly what I need. Grabbing me by the hips, he pulls me back onto his throbbing member, his rhythm changing from a slow tease to something rougher, more primal. He bucks into me like a wild animal, and the force of it is enough to drive me over the edge again.

The climax slams into me, hard and fast, and I'm completely wrecked. I cry out, my body trembling as he keeps driving into me, making sure I feel every last bit of him. He's relentless, pounding into my slick pussy until I'm seeing stars and left breathless and utterly satisfied.

He's holding me from behind, his touch like a magic eraser, wiping away all the stress from the day. His lips trail kisses along my shoulder, then down my back, each one making me feel a little more at ease, a little more cherished.

His voice breaks through my thoughts. "What do you want, Willow?"

I know exactly what I want. "I want you in bed, on top of me. I want you to fuck me until you come deep inside me."

He grins, that sexy, cocky grin, and then he's kissing me, long and deep, like he's got all the time in the world. It's not just a kiss; it's a promise, and it makes my heart do a weird little flip.

He helps me out of the tub, and I watch as he wraps a towel around his waist, the muscles in his arms flexing. Then he's drying me off, so gentle, like he's taking his time, like he's savoring every moment. He pushes me down onto the bed and climbs on top of me, and instinctively, I spread my legs, already desperate to feel him inside me again.

He presses the head of his cock against my clit, rubbing it just enough to make me moan. My hips buck up, wanting more, but he holds back, making me wait.

"You feel so damn good," he murmurs, his voice low and rough. "I can't stop thinking about being inside you."

My heart skips a beat, and I feel my cheeks flush. "Same," I whisper, almost breathless, as his teasing gets me all worked up. The anticipation is killing me, and he knows it.

He keeps playing with me, the tip of his cock sliding against me just enough to make my body ache for more. Finally, when I'm about ready to lose my mind, he reaches down, takes his cock in his hand, and slides it inside me, nice and slow.

It's like everything falls into place—he fits so perfectly, stretching me just right, filling me up in a way that makes my whole body sing. All I can do is smile, pure happiness spreading through me as he starts to move, and everything else just fades away.

It's just us, just this moment, and damn, it feels so good.

Every nerve in my body is lighting up. He's slow at first, deliberate, each thrust hitting my G spot and making me moan. The pleasure is intense, but there's something else there too—something softer, more tender.

"You feel so good," he murmurs, his voice thick with emotion.. " I could stay inside you forever, just like this. You're everything I want, everything I need."

His words wrap around me, making my heart pound in a way that's more than just lust.

Is this love?

Are we making love?

The thought stirs something deep inside me, something warm and overwhelming. It feels so right, so real, but I bite my tongue, holding back the words threatening to spill out. The last thing I want is to freak him out by getting too serious too fast.

Instead, I focus on the moment, wrapping my legs around his hips and pulling him deeper inside me. He groans, his breath hot against my neck, and I can feel him tense, the rhythm of his thrusts growing faster, more urgent.

I dig my nails into his back, leaning up to whisper in his ear, "I'm ready to come, just for you."

And we're both there. The orgasm hits us at the same time, and it's like everything else disappears. His cock pulses deep inside me, filling me up as we come together, hard and fast. I can feel him draining every last drop inside, and it's the most intense, perfect release I could've imagined. We're breathless, totally spent, and I'm left with this crazy, overwhelming sense of satisfaction.

He leans down, his lips meeting mine in a soft, lingering kiss, so different from the intensity we just shared. "You're so beautiful. ," he murmurs, his voice low and full of something I can't quite place. "So damn sexy when you come."

I grin, playfully arching a brow. "Only when I come?"

He chuckles, shaking his head. "You have no idea," he says, his tone teasing but with an edge of seriousness that makes my heart skip a beat.."

He pulls me close, his arms wrapping around me as he kisses my forehead, then my shoulders, each touch making me feel all warm and fuzzy inside. *What's going on?* I wonder, my thoughts spinning. *Is he falling for me, too? Or am I just reading too much into this?*

For a moment, I feel like I should tell him. The words are right there, the other secret I've been carrying around. But before I can decide if I'm actually going to say it, he pulls back slightly, giving me a look that reminds me we're not playing house here.

"You know you can't sleep in bed with me," he says, his tone casual but firm.

I try to play it cool, but there's a pang of something that feels a lot like rejection.

"Yeah, I haven't forgotten."

It's just sex, after all.

CHAPTER 18

"You alright?"

For a split second, it looks like Willow's about to... *cry?*

My gut tightens. But she pulls herself together, throwing on the brave face she wears so well.

"Yeah, I'm fine," she says, brushing it off.

I lean in, kissing her shoulder, breathing in her scent. It's intoxicating, floating through me like a drug. "It's for the best we don't share a bed," I speak against her skin.

I mean it, too. Keeping things separate is how we avoid complicating this arrangement.

She nods, but there's something in her eyes, a flicker of something I can't quite read. "Yeah, it is. I know."

She rolls out of bed, and I can't help but watch as she bends over to pick up her panties. The way her body moves, the curve of her hips—fuck, she's sexy as hell. My eyes roam over her, and before I know it, I'm hard again. I want her, all over again, like I haven't just had her.

She slips on her panties, and I'm biting back the urge to pull her back into bed, to forget about the rules we've set up. But I hold back, keeping my distance, even as every part of me is screaming to take her again. This thing between us—it's dangerous, but damn if it doesn't feel right.

She turns around, standing in front of me in just her panties, and my eyes immediately lock onto her pink nipples, still firm from our time together. The memory of their taste is fresh in my mouth, and I feel another surge of desire.

"Can I use the gym again in the morning?" she asks, her tone casual with a hint of an edge.

"Of course," I say, my voice smooth. "I'll even do breakfast for the girls if you want to take your time."

She gives me a polite smile, shaking her head. "Thanks, but I won't shirk my responsibilities."

I watch her as she starts getting dressed, and the urge to know more about her, beyond what she shows me, nags at me. "Can I ask you something?"

She pauses, her fingers on her bra strap, and looks at me with caution. "What's that?"

"Do you have big plans for your yoga?" I ask, and I can see the wheels turning in her head as she considers the question.

She's wearing nothing but her bra and panties, and she's a vision of temptation, but I'm after something deeper.

"Maybe one day," she says, slipping into her clothes.

I watch her, my curiosity piqued more than ever.

"I'll see you in the morning," I tell her. "Have a good workout."

She hesitates, like there's something else she wants to say. I wait, but she just nods, offering a simple "Good night," before heading out. The room feels different once she's gone, quieter, but not in a way that brings any peace.

I roll over in bed, hands behind my head, staring at the ceiling. There's no doubt in my mind that she's hiding something, some kind of secret she's not ready to share. Maybe she's starting to have second thoughts about all of this, about us. But then again, the way she responded to me, the way her body reacted, it didn't feel like someone who wanted out.

Maybe she wants more. That's always been a risk, and the truth is, it's a risk I'm starting to think I might be willing to take. The scary part is realizing I might feel the same way, that maybe this isn't just about sex anymore.

I think back to how happy the girls were when she came home earlier, how they lit up around her. It's not just about her and me—it's about them, too.

Whatever she's holding back, I need to get to the bottom of it. I need to know what's going on in her head, and whether it could change everything for us.

She's got secrets, and I want to know every last one of them.

❦

Flashes of last night flood my mind—the way Willow moaned, her voice breathless and needy, the look on her face as I drove deep inside her. I can still feel the way she clenched around me, her pussy gripping me tight as she came hard, her body shaking with the intensity of it.

The memory alone is enough to make my cock ache with need, waking me up hard as a rock. I roll over, half expecting to see her beside me, but the bed is empty. The sheets are cold where she should be. I never thought I'd want someone next to me when I woke up, but damn, I wish she was here. Not just for the sex, though God knows I want that too—badly.

The idea of waking up next to her, holding her close, kissing her awake, whispering a lazy "good morning" into her ear... It's more appealing than I'd ever admit out loud.

But she's not here. Just like we agreed. No overnights, no lingering, no getting too close.

I sigh, trying to push the thoughts away as I glance at the clock. It's time to get up, time to start the day. The empty space beside me, where she should be, nags at me, reminding me that maybe this whole thing isn't as simple as I thought it could be.

I roll out of bed and head straight for the shower, the hot water washing away the sweat from last night. As much as I like the idea of her scent lingering on me, I know it would be too much of a distraction, especially with all the thoughts swirling in my head. The water cascades down, but it does nothing to cool the heat that's building again.

My cock gets hard as hell as I flash back to her on her knees, her lips wrapped around me, taking me deep, the way she looked up at me with those eyes, full of need. Part of me wants to finish myself off, but I grit my teeth and think better of it. I don't want that. I want her.

I hop out of the shower, towel off, and get dressed; my mind still tangled up in thoughts of her. I start thinking about how I'd like to spend the day with Willow and the girls, maybe take them Christmas shopping, let the girls pick out some things they want. It sounds... nice. Maybe even more than nice. It sounds like something a family would do.

Just then my phone buzzes on the counter, snapping me out of my thoughts. A text. I grab the phone, my jaw tightening as I swipe to see it's from Sal.

On my way over. Something important we need to discuss ASAP—in person and in private.

I text Sal back: *I'm ready. Come over.*

He responds almost immediately: *Need to park in the garage. We'll need to use the basement.*

I know what that means—this isn't just a casual drop-by. Whatever Sal has found, it's big, and it needs to be handled quietly and out of sight.

I head downstairs, and the smell of coffee and pancakes hits me before I even reach the kitchen. When I step inside, I catch sight of Willow at the stove, flipping pancakes while the girls chatter around her.

It's a scene I could get used to, something simple and perfect. For a second, I wish I could just stay here, at this moment.

Willow glances up and smiles when she sees me. "Morning. Want some coffee?"

"Morning. ," I reply, my tone warm but distracted. "Wish I could, but I've got something I need to take care of." I glance at the girls. "Last day of preschool before Christmas break, right?"

"Nope!" Giulia says. "No school today!"

"Is that right?"

"The news says lots of snow," Lucia says.

Willow jumps in. "And that means the break starts today."

A tinge of tension runs through me. I'd hoped to have the house to myself for the day with the business I need to attend to.

"Don't worry," Willow says. "I'll be getting the girls out of the house before the snow starts. Get them a little fresh air and sunshine before a potential snow-in."

"Sounds good," I reply. It's like she's able to read my mind.

The girls look up from their plates, their faces full of questions, but before I can say more, the chime rings through the house, signaling Sal's arrival.

"Are you expecting someone?" Willow asks as she flips another pancake.

"Just business," I say, trying to keep it light. "I'll be back soon."

She nods, her eyes searching mine for a second before she turns back to the stove. "Alright. We'll save you some breakfast."

I give her a quick nod. "Thanks. I'll see you in a bit."

I pull out my phone and hit the button on the security app to let him in. My mind is already shifting gears, preparing for whatever Sal may have found.

Just as I'm about to open the door to the garage, it swings open on its own. Sal's already there, his usual confident grin on his face. He's in his late thirties, built like a damn tank, with a jawline sharp enough to cut glass. His tailored suit hugs his frame just right, and his eyes are sharp, always calculating.

"Thought I'd say hi to the girls first," Sal says.

"Of course," I reply, even though I'm eager to get to the matter at hand. The girls love their Uncle Sal, and I can't deny them a few minutes with him.

We head into the kitchen, and as soon as the girls see him, they spring out of their seats like they've been shot out of a cannon. "Uncle Sal!" they squeal in unison, rushing over to him. He bends down, arms wide, catching them both in a big hug.

"There's my favorite girls!" he says, lifting them off the ground easily. "You two getting into trouble, or just giving your dad a hard time?"

They giggle, clinging to him like they've just found treasure. The girls love Sal. It's always like this when Sal's around.

He straightens, turning his attention to Willow. "And who's this lovely lady?" he asks, his tone smooth as silk.

"Willow," she introduces herself, offering a polite smile. "I'm the new nanny."

"Willow, huh?" Sal says, flashing his best charming grin. "Beautiful name for a beautiful woman."

She laughs, but I feel an intense rush of jealousy spike through me. I know Sal's a shameless flirt but seeing him work his charm on her grates on me.

"Alright, Sal," I cut in. , my voice firm. "Time to get to work."

Sal meets my eyes and nods, understanding the fun's over. "Lead the way, boss."

Sal and I head down to the garage. "What's going on? What'd you find?"

Sal glances at me, his expression serious. "I found a guy that knows who killed your father and his associates."

His words stop me cold. My blood turns to ice, every nerve in my body on high alert. "Where is he?"

Sal grins the kind of grin that usually means he's got something good. "He's in my trunk."

A sharp, almost disbelieving laugh escapes me as we walk to his car—a sleek, black Audi S7, functional but eye-catching enough to turn heads. He pops open the trunk, and there's a guy inside, looking like he's been through hell and back. His face is bruised, his clothes torn, and he's bound tight, barely able to move.

The sight of him stirs something dark in me—a need for answers, for justice. For revenge. I step closer, my eyes narrowing as I take in the pathetic sight before me.

"You've got some explaining to do. ," I say, my voice cold and hard as steel. "And I suggest you start fast, if you want to leave here in one piece."

The guy mumbles through the gag, his eyes wide with fear. I can tell he's begging for his life—they always do. I smirk, knowing exactly how this is going to play out.

"Sal, take this prick to the basement."

Sal nods, and we both know what's coming next. Attached to the garage is a separate door that leads to the sound-proofed basement, which is perfect for the kind of conversation I'm about to have. It's where the real work gets done, where the truth comes out one way or another.

"I'll be right there," I tell Sal, watching as he hauls the guy out of the trunk and drags him toward the door. The guy's struggling, but it's pointless. He's got nowhere to run.

I take a deep breath and head back into the house. Willow and the girls are still in the kitchen, chatting and eating breakfast. It's a peaceful scene, the kind that almost makes me forget what I'm about to do.

Almost.

"I'll be working downstairs," I tell Willow, my tone casual..

"Sure," she says, but I can see it in her eyes—she knows something more is going on. She's not stupid. But she doesn't press, just nods, her gaze lingering on me a moment longer than usual.

As I head back down, I can't help but wonder just how much she knows about what I do for a living. And more importantly, what she'd say if she knew all the grisly details.

Would she still look at me the same way? Or would it change everything?

The thought nags at me as I approach the storage room in the basement, ready to do some dirty work.

CHAPTER 19

WILLOW

"Willow, do you know where Mr. Conti is?" Ms. M. walks into the kitchen, her usual calm and collected self.

I'm wiping down the table, clearing away the last of the girls' breakfast. "He said he'll be in the basement."

She pauses, just for a second, but it's enough to catch my attention. Something about that makes her uneasy.

"What's going on?" I ask, my curiosity kicking in..

Ms. M glances at the girls, who are busy pulling on their coats and boots, completely oblivious. She lowers her voice, almost like she's letting me in on a secret.

"He doesn't usually bring his work home."

I frown, not sure what to make of that. "What kind of work?"

She gives me a tight, polite smile, the kind that says she knows way more than she's letting on. "You don't need to worry about any of that, dear. It's better that way."

She turns and leaves, her heels clicking as she walks away. I'm left standing there, dish towel in hand, feeling a wave of confusion. What exactly is happening in the basement right now? I try to shake it off, telling myself it's none of my business, but the questions keep nagging at me.

I know Nico's involved with the Mob somehow, but the details are fuzzy. I don't know exactly what he does, how high up he is, or if he's just the public face for whatever shady stuff goes down. Part of me wants to dig deeper, to really understand the man I'm falling for.

The other part? It's telling me to let it lie for my own good. I'm torn.

Before I can dwell on it too much, the girls come bouncing back into the kitchen, all bundled up in their coats, gloves, and hats. They're practically buzzing with excitement.

"Can we go to Central Park, Willow?" Giulia asks, her eyes wide with hope.. "Instead of just the backyard?"

I check my phone for the weather. "It's supposed to get really snowy in a bit," I tell them. "So yeah, we can go, but we can't stay out too late."

The girls cheer like I've just told them they won the lottery. Their energy is infectious, and for a moment, all the questions about Nico and his world fade into the background.

We head over to Central Park, and the city's looking like a whole winter wonderland. Snow's just starting to fall, making everything all picturesque and cozy. The girls are hyped, pointing out every cute shop we pass, begging to go in and look for presents.

"Park first, shopping later," I tell them, laughing when they give me those big puppy eyes.. "We'll grab some hot chocolate after, and then maybe we can hit the shops – assuming the weather isn't too bad."

That does the trick, and soon we're strolling into the park, heading toward Shakespeare Garden on the Upper West Side. The place is straight-up magical, with snow covering the trees and pathways. The girls waste no time—they're off, throwing snowballs and making snow angels like it's the best day of their lives.

I plop down on a bench, trying to relax, but of course, my brain's stuck on Nico. What kind of work is he doing in that basement? Money laundering? Drug deals? Or something even darker?

Before I can spiral too hard, I spot Lucia climbing a massive rock.

"Lucia, get down from there!" I yell.

She's wobbling like she's about to fall.

"Shit!" I mutter, jumping off the bench. I rush over, trying to catch her, but I'm too late. She slips and falls, smacking her head on the base of the rock. A trickle of blood appears. The second Lucia sees the blood, she starts screaming like it's the end of the world. And of course, that sets off Giulia, who starts screaming too.

I kneel, checking the injury. It doesn't look too bad—just a small cut, really—but I can't tell if it needs stitches or not.

My heart's pounding, and I'm trying to stay calm, but I can feel the panic creeping in.

I whip out my phone and fire off a text to Ms. M, snapping a quick pic of Lucia's cut and letting her know what's up.

Lucia had a little fall, cut her head. Not sure if it needs stitches, but we're heading home now.

I quickly gather the girls, trying to calm them down. My mind's racing, fear running through me. My heart's pounding like crazy as I hurry home with the girls. What if Lucia has a concussion? My mind's spiraling with all the worst-case scenarios.

Every few minutes, I ask Lucia how she feels, and she keeps saying, "I'm okay," but there's this dazed look in her eyes that's freaking me out.

We finally make it back to the house, and I rush Lucia to the bathroom to clean up her cut. I'm practically shaking as I turn on the faucet, gently washing away the blood.

Just as I'm about to grab a towel, Ms. M appears in the doorway., her face full of concern. "How did this happenWhat happened?" she asks, hurrying over to us.

"She fell off a rock in the park," I explain, my voice a little shaky. "I'm worried it might be more than a little cut."

Ms. M takes a quick look at Lucia's head, then checks her pupils with a calm efficiency I'm seriously grateful for. "Let's just let her rest and keep an eye on her," she says, her tone reassuring.

I nod, trying to take a deep breath as we guide Lucia to the couch. At least Ms. M is here to help—I don't know what I'd do without her right now.

Giulia's hovering close, her little face scrunched up with worry. "Is Lucia really hurt?" she asks, her voice trembling.

Ms. M gives her a comforting smile. "She's going to be just fine, sweetie. We just need to clean her up a bit." Then she glances at me. "Willow, can you grab some antiseptic?"

"On it," I say, giving Lucia's hand a quick squeeze before hurrying out of the room.

CHAPTER 20

NICO

I'm standing outside the door to the storage room. I'm focused. Inside, Sal's doing his thing, giving the poor shithead the introductory round of persuasion.

We've perfected the routine over the years—Sal comes in swinging, softening them up, and then I step in, giving them a final chance to talk before I get creative.

The room's completely soundproof, so I can't hear a damn thing from where I'm standing, but I know the drill. The only sounds in my head are the ticking of the clock and the low hum of adrenaline, sharpening my senses. This is business, pure and simple.

Finally, the door swings open, and Sal steps out, wiping blood off his knuckles with a rag. His face is set in a grim line. "Fucker's not talking," he says., frustration seeping into his voice. "If I work his face over any more, his jaw's gonna be too busted to use."

I nod, the cold calculation settling in. This is my cue. Sal's done his part, and now it's my turn to finish the job. I crack my knuckles, the familiar anticipation buzzing through me.

"Leave it to me," I say, my tone steady, controlled. ."

Sal steps aside, giving me a look that says he knows exactly what's coming next. I push the door open, ready to make this bastard talk.

Sal nods toward the stairs. "I'm gonna wash up, make a few calls to the other lieutenants."

I give him a quick nod, watching as he heads out. I turn back to the door, taking a moment to steel myself before stepping inside. The door shuts behind me with a heavy click, sealing us off from the outside world.

The room is our little slice of hell, and I'm about to drag this poor bastard right into the middle of it.

The man in the chair is slumped over, breathing hard, his face a bloody mess.

"Welcome to my little workshop," I say, my voice low and almost friendly as I circle him. "You're probably noticing a few things about this room. For starters, it's soundproof—no one's going to hear a thing, no matter how loud you scream."

I let the words sink in, watching as the man's eyes dart around, taking in his surroundings. "Those doors are solid steel, thick enough to keep anyone out—or in. We've got security cameras rolling, so every single moment gets captured. And that drain over there in the corner?" I nod toward it, my smile widening. "That's for easy cleaning when things get messy."

I pause, leaning in close. "So, let's get started, shall we?"

I step closer to the man, sizing him up. He's in his thirties, longish hair matted with sweat and streaked with blood. His once-fancy suit is now a mess, covered in scuffs and splatters, the kind of designer outfit that screams money and status. His fingers are adorned with expensive rings, and there's a flashy watch on his wrist. None of that impresses me.

What catches my attention is the sheer terror in his eyes.

I look him up and down, taking my time. "You know, " I start, my voice calm, almost conversational, "you don't strike me as a killer. You're too prissy." I lean in closer. ", making sure he knows I see right through him. "You're just a spoiled little shit who's in way over his head."

He squirms in the chair, his eyes wide as he tries to scream through the gag. The bindings are tight, cutting into his skin, and he's trembling so hard I'm half-expecting him to piss his pants any second now.

"Here's how this is going to work," I say, my tone dropping an octave. "You're going to give me the information I need. Whether you leave here with all your limbs and fingers intact? That's up to you."

His panic intensifies, his muffled screams growing louder. I watch him struggle, a pathetic sight, really.

"I'm going to remove your gag now," I continue, my voice steady, "and when I do, I expect you to start talking."

I reach out and yank the gag off, and the man immediately lets out a blood-curdling scream. Without missing a beat, I backhand him hard across the face, the sound of the slap echoing in the room. The scream dies in his throat, replaced by a whimper as he looks up at me with fear-filled eyes.

"Now, ," I say, my voice cold and commanding. "Let's try that again. Talk."

The guy coughs and sputters, looking up at me. "I don't know anything about your goddamn dad."

I nod slowly, letting his words hang in the air for a moment. Then, without warning, I rush forward and grab him by his long hair, yanking it back hard. His head snaps back, and he lets out a strained yell of pain.

"You're in my house now," I growl, my voice low and menacing. "And while you're here, you're going to speak to me with a little more respect. You'll call me Mr. Conti, and you'll keep that tone of yours in check."

He groans, his face contorted in agony, but he stays silent. I keep my grip on his hair, making sure he understands just how serious I am. "Remember what I said about your limbs and fingers," I continue. "You'd do well to keep that in mind."

I release him, and he slumps back in the chair, breathing heavily. For a moment, there's nothing but the sound of his ragged breaths filling the room. Finally, he speaks, his voice trembling. "I didn't kill your father."

I clear my throat, a warning in the sound. His eyes flicker with fear, and he quickly corrects himself. "I didn't kill your father, Mr. Conti."

I nod slowly, my expression unreadable. "Good. Now, what's your name?"

"Jack," he answers, his voice barely above a whisper.

"Alright, Jack," I say, my tone still commanding. "Let's see if you've got anything else worth telling me."

Jack's eyes dart around, desperate. "I don't know anything.", he stammers, but I can see through the lie.

I step closer. "You're bullshitting me. I know you've got some information—don't bother trying to deny it. I can tell."

Jack's eyes widen in fear. , but he sticks to his story. "You're wrong," he insists, but the tremor in his voice betrays him.."

Without another word, I walk slowly over to the wall of the room, my steps measured. There's a barely noticeable compartment there, one only I know how to open. I press on it, revealing a hidden set of surgical implements. The sight of them makes Jack's breath hitch, and he starts to struggle against his restraints, but it's no use.

I run my fingers over the tools, letting the moment drag out. "You know, it's such a cliché for men like me to use their fists, to hack off fingers, to break kneecaps," I say, my tone conversational. "And honestly, it's inefficient. People pass out from the pain before they spill a word."

I glance back at Jack, and his eyes are locked on the array of gleaming instruments, his terror palpable. I grin, picking up a small scalpel from the rack, turning it over in my hand. "Over the years, I've learned to be a little more... precise with my interrogation techniques."

I step closer, holding the scalpel up for him to see. The sharp edge catches the light, glinting ominously. "Now, Jack," I say, my voice dropping to a whisper. "Let's see if this doesn't jog your memory."

I move, yanking Jack's hair back again and pressing the tip of the scalpel against his throat. Just enough to draw a bead of blood, a tiny red dot that stands out against his pale skin. "Talk," I growl, my voice cold and lethal.

Jack's eyes widen, but he surprises me. "Or what?" he spits back, his voice trembling but defiant. "You'll cut my throat? You'll get nothing that way."

I'm taken aback for a split second. The guy looked soft, like he'd crumble the moment things got real. But now, with a blade at his throat, he's showing some spine. There's clearly more to him than meets the eye.

And he's not wrong—this guy is our first real lead, and if I end him now, we're back to square one.

I let him go, releasing my grip on his hair and stepping back. His chest heaves as he catches his breath, the small cut on his throat starting to trickle blood down to his collar. I return to the rack of medical implements, my mind racing. The scalpel feels too final, too crude for what I need right now.

I set it aside, letting my eyes roam over the array of tools, thinking about my next move. One way or another, I'm going to get the information I need out of him. Whether it's through fear, pain, or something else entirely, this guy is going to talk. It's just a matter of time.

A grin spreads across my face as my eyes land on just the right tool—a wireless, electric bone saw. I take it from its place, turning toward Jack and revving it up, the blade spinning with a high-pitched whir. The sound alone is enough to send chills down anyone's spine, and I make sure Jack gets a good look at it.

"You know what this is?" I ask, my voice calm, almost casual. "It's a bone saw. Incredibly efficient at doing what it needs to do. Sure, smashing fingers with a mallet gets the job done, but this? This is cleaner. Faster."

Jack's trying to keep it together, but I can see the sweat beading on his forehead, the way his eyes widen with fear, the early brief flash of defiance gone. He's on the edge of breaking.

I step closer, the saw buzzing in my hand. "We'll start small," I say, my tone almost reassuring, like I'm doing him a favor.. " Just your pinky."

Before he can protest, I grab his hand and tie it down onto the arm of the chair, making sure he can't move. The saw hums as I press the blade against his finger, just enough to let him feel the cold metal..

Jack's composure shatters. He squeals, thrashing against his restraints, yelling.

"Stop! Stop! Stop!" over and over, desperation lacing his voice.

I pause, my finger hovering over the trigger. "Who killed my father?" I ask, my voice deadly serious.

He's trembling, his voice shaking as he finally cracks. "I've heard a couple of names," he stammers.."

"Good," I say, pulling the saw back slightly. "What names?"

"Antonio and Marco Rossi," Jack says.

I know the names. They're low-level guys in the Rossi crime family, the kind of bottom feeders who handle small-time jobs, not something as big as taking out my father and his associates. This smells like bullshit.

"That's all I know,"." Jack insists, desperation creeping into his voice.

I narrow my eyes at him, considering my next move.. "Was the hit on my father and his men ordered by the Rossis?"

Jack clams up, refusing to answer, his eyes darting away. Without hesitation, I calmly punch him in the mouth, the force snapping his head back. He groans in pain, blood trickling from his split lip as he struggles to refocus.

When he finally does, I ask again, "What's your relationship to the Rossis?"

Jack spits out some blood, grimacing. "I'm a numbers guy."

"You mean a money launderer," I correct, my tone icy.."

"Yeah, whatever," Jack mutters, clearly realizing there's no point in lying.."

I lean in close, grinning as I let the next question roll off my tongue. "Tell me, Jack, is that a job you can do without your fingers?"

Jack's eyes widen with terror, and he screams, the sound echoing in the cold, sterile room.

CHAPTER 21

WILLOW

I'm sitting in the living room with Lucia and Giulia, both of them huddled together on the edge of the couch. They're holding each other's hands, Giulia whispering, "You're gonna be okay, Lucia," over and over, like she's trying to will it into reality.

Lucia's still sniffling as Ms. M gently dabs the cut on her head with a damp washcloth, trying to be careful. The wound looks red and swollen, and though it's not gushing blood anymore, it doesn't look pretty either. I hand her the antiseptic and she gingerly dabs it on the cut while Lucia squirms and hisses at the burning. sensation.

Ms. M inspects it closely, pursing her lips. "Now that it's all cleaned out, I think it might actually need a couple stitches," she says finally, her voice steady.."

I nod, feeling a little more relieved that Ms. M is taking charge. She always seems to know what to do. The girls look at us with wide, anxious eyes, and I do my best to smile.

"Don't worry, Lu. We've got you."

Ms. M gently guides me to the other side of the room, away from the girls. Lucia's still sniffling, but Giulia's doing her best to comfort her.

"There's a clinic a couple blocks down," Ms. M says quietly. , her tone is all business. "We can take Lucia there, have them check if she needs stitches."

I nod, feeling a bit better about the plan. "Yeah, good idea. We'll just tell Mr. Conti, then head out."

As soon as I mention Nico, the color seems to drain from Ms. M's face. It's quick, and she's a pro at pulling herself together, but I notice.

"No, no," she says, almost too quickly. "We'll tell him later."

I blink, confused. "Won't he want to know what happened? I mean, she's his daughter."

Ms. M's expression tightens, and she lowers her voice even more. "We'll tell him after. He's never to be disturbed when he brings his work home. He's made this point very clear. And I have authorization to take the girls in for any medical needs."

I don't like this—it doesn't sit right with me. "I'm not cool with this, Ms. M.," I say, crossing my arms. "Nico would want to know if something happened to one of his little girls."

Ms. M's face sharpens, her usual calm demeanor turning icy. "I know what Mr. Conti would want, Willow. He is not to be disturbed while he's working."

I shake my head. , not buying it. "No way. He'd want to know his daughter got hurt. This isn't something you keep from a parent."

Ms. M narrows her eyes, clearly not happy with my push back. s. "I appreciate your concern, but Mr. Conti has strict rules. He doesn't like being interrupted, and for good reason."

I feel my frustration bubbling over. "This isn't just a papercut, Ms. M. She has a gash on her head. What if she has a concussion? You don't think he'll be mad if we don't tell him immediately? I'm going to go tell him."

"Willow, don't!" Ms. M calls after me.

But I'm already moving quickly down the hall. If Nico's doing something so important that he can't be bothered about his own kid's injury, I want to hear it from him directly.

I make my way to the basement stairs, the darkness swallowing me as I descend. My footsteps echo in the silence. It's eerily quiet down here, and my gut tightens with unease.

Something on the floor catches my eye and I walk over to get a better look.

Blood.

A dark, wet stain on the cold concrete floor. I gasp, my heart racing, a mix of fear and dread washing over me.. What the hell is going on down here? Suddenly, all the warnings and the fear in Ms. M's eyes make sense, but it's too late—I'm already in too deep.

I freeze when I hear a voice. My heart skips a beat, and I pull back into the shadows, trying to make myself as invisible as possible. It's Sal, and he's on the phone with someone. His tone is serious, clipped, and even though I can't make out every word, a few hit me hard.

"Killer," he says, the word slicing through the silence. Then something about "Mr. Conti getting information out of him."

My mind races, piecing it together faster than I want to admit. This isn't just some meeting or business deal. Nico's down here doing something dark, something dangerous. I'm not supposed to be here, and I know it, but I can't stop myself from finding out what's going on.

I spot a door on the other side of the room. Keeping low, I creep over to it, my breath shaky. With a quick glance back at Sal to make sure he's not looking, I slowly turn the handle and slip through.

The door opens into a sleek, stainless-steel hallway, cold and clinical, like something out of a movie.

Every instinct in me is *screaming* to turn back, to get the hell out of here before I see something I can't unsee. I've known, on some level, what kind of man Nico is, but now I'm about to find out for real. My feet feel like they're made of lead, but I keep moving forward anyway, even as my heart races with dread.

In the distance, I can faintly hear Ms. M talking to Sal somewhere behind me, though their words are muffled, indistinct.

It's now or never.

I force myself to the end of the hallway and push open the door. The sight that greets me makes my stomach lurch.

A man is strapped to a chair, bloodied and battered, looking like he's been through hell. Nico is standing over him, holding a large surgical instrument against the man's pinky finger. Blood seeps from a fresh wound, dripping onto the cold floor.

The man's eyes lock onto mine, and he calls out, desperation thick in his voice. "Help me!" he pleads, his voice raw.

Nico's head snaps toward the door, and our eyes meet. This isn't the Nico I know—the caring father, the man I've been falling for.

This is someone else entirely, someone terrifying.

I gasp, my breath catching in my throat, and without another thought, I turn and bolt back down the hall and up the stairs, fleeing from the nightmare unfolding behind me.

CHAPTER 22

NICO

I wince, the image of Willow's horrified face seared into my mind like a brand. The way she looked at me—like I was a monster—burns deep, and I know I'll never forget it.

She's long gone by now, and there's a knot in my gut telling me she's not coming back. Can't say I'd blame her if she didn't.

I take a breath, trying to push the emotions down. I turn to Jack, who's whimpering in the chair, and say, "You just got lucky. For now." My voice is cold, detached, but inside I'm anything but. I step out of the room, shutting the door behind me, blocking out Jack's muffled cries.

In the hallway, Sal and Ms. M rush toward me, both of them looking like they'd seen a ghost. Sal's the first to speak. "I was on the phone, boss. I didn't see her."

Ms. M. is more frantic, her usual calm shattered. "I tried to stop her, Mr. Conti. I swear, I tried!"

I hold up a hand to silence them, my mind racing. The damage is done, and I don't need excuses right now. Willow's seen the truth—the part of me I've kept hidden from her, from the girls. And now? Now I have to figure out what the hell I'm going to do about it.

"Where is she?" I ask, my voice tight, trying to keep it together. Because if I don't find her, if she's out there running with that look of horror in her eyes, I'm not sure I'll ever be able to make this right.

I'm halfway to the stairs when I realize I'm still holding the damn bone saw. I hand it to Sal, who takes it without a word.

"Stay with Jack," I tell him, my voice clipped and controlled.

Sal nods, all business. "I'm on it."

I turn to Ms. M, walking beside her as we head upstairs. There's a tightness in my chest, but I push it down, focusing on the here and now. "Why was she downstairs? What's so important that she broke the rule and came down while I was working?"

Her face is pale, her voice trembling slightly as she answers. "Lucia fell at the park and hit her head."

Everything else fades in an instant. My heart lurches. "Where is she?" I demand, every other concern shoved to the back of my mind.

"Upstairs," Ms. M says quickly. "Willow wanted to tell you before we took her to the clinic to be looked at."

She's still talking, explaining, but all I can think about is Lucia. My little girl, hurt and needing me. Nothing else matters right now.

"I told them to wait in the den," Ms. M says, her voice steadying when she realizes my focus has shifted.

I don't wait for more. I rush forward, all thoughts of Willow, of the mess downstairs, gone. All that matters is getting to my little girls, making sure Lucia is okay.

I stop short, realizing there's still blood on my hands. The sight of it makes my stomach turn, a reminder of how close my worlds are to colliding. I head to the sink, scrubbing the blood away, watching it swirl down the drain. It's not just the blood of the man downstairs—it's the blood of the life I've tried to keep separate from my girls.

This was bound to happen. Deep down, I always knew it was inevitable. But now that it's here, all I can do is hope my girls never learn the truth about who I am—what I do. They deserve better than that.

I take a deep breath, composing myself before heading into the den. As soon as I step inside, a wave of relief washes over me. Willow is there. I should've known she wouldn't abandon the girls, no matter what she saw.

She's kneeling by Lucia, gently tending to the wound on her forehead. My heart clenches at the sight of my daughter, but she looks better than I feared. The fact that she's up and moving is a good sign.

As soon as the girls spot me, they light up, rushing over and throwing their arms around me. I drop to a knee and hug them tight, feeling Lucia's little arms around my neck, and for a moment, everything else fades away. At least she's okay, and that's all that matters right now.

I gently tell Lucia to step back so I can get a good look at the wound. It's a nasty gash, but I keep my voice calm as I say.

"It's not as bad as it looks. Head wounds bleed a lot, even when they're not too serious." I notice Willow tense, like she's suddenly realizing how I might know so much about injuries like this.

Ms. M enters the room. "I wanted to take them to the clinic right away," she says, glancing at Willow.

Willow nods, still looking a little shaken. "I just wanted to make sure you knew what was going on," she adds, her voice quiet but firm.

I nod, appreciating both of their instincts. "I trust both of you," I say, making it clear I wouldn't have been upset if Ms. M had just taken them. "But thank you, Willow, for wanting to keep me in the loop."

I shift my attention back to Lucia, her little hand still gripping mine. "We're going to the clinic now," I say, my tone leaving no room for argument. I stand up, ready to move, then turn to Willow. "I want you to come with us."

She nods, her eyes meeting mine with a mix of emotions—relief, fear, and something else I can't quite place. But now's not the time to dwell on it.

Right now, I need to make sure my little girl gets the care she needs.

Lucia looks up at me, her eyes a little unfocused, and says, "Daddy, I feel dizzy."

A spike of worry shoots through me. Her eyes don't look quite right, and dizziness is a serious red flag—she might have a concussion. I don't want to scare her, so my voice is calm and gentle. "The doctor at the clinic will fix you right up," I say, already thinking about the quickest way to get her to the clinic.

I turn to Ms. M, who's hovering nearby, concern etched on her face. "Get the car ready."

"Of course," she replies, and without another word, she hurries off to do as I've asked.

I lead Willow and the girls into the kitchen, but I can see how tense Willow is around me, like she's bracing herself for something bad. It guts me that she feels this way, but I can't blame her after what she saw.

"Tell me what happened," I ask, looking at Willow for confirmation.

"Lucia was climbing a rock at the park and lost her balance."

"Willow told me to get down, but I didn't want to," Lucia confesses.

"We'll talk about that later," I say. to her.

As I step outside, Ms. M is pulling up in the Lexus SUV, the engine purring quietly. I carry Lucia close to my chest. Her little arms are wrapped around my neck, and I can feel how light and fragile she is at this moment. It tears at something deep inside me, but I push it down, focusing on getting her taken care of.

Willow helps Giulia into the car while I carefully strap Lucia into her seat. The sight of her with that wound on her head, looking so small and vulnerable, twists a knife in my gut. But I have to stay composed, for her sake.

"You're going to be fine, baby," I tell her, brushing a hand gently over her hair.

Lucia looks up at me, her voice small. "Are you coming, Papa?"

I frown. I have to get to Sal, tell him to take that son of bitch somewhere else. But I need to go with Lucia.

Ms. M sees my struggle and says, "Don't worry. I can handle it until you get there."

I force a reassuring smile when I look at Lucia. "Alright there, sweetheart. I just need to check in with Uncle Sal first."

Willow says nothing, but I catch the look in her eyes—she knows exactly what I mean by "check in with Sal." She knows I need to wrap up whatever unfinished business I have in the basement. She climbs into the front seat without speaking.

I close the car door gently, then turn to Ms. M. "Text me when you get there," I instruct her.."

She nods, and without another word, she pulls away from the curb and into the street, heading toward the clinic. I watch them go for a moment, a heavy weight settling in my chest, before turning back toward the house.

I look up at the sky, noticing the dark clouds rolling in, turning a mean shade of gray. A hell of a storm is coming, and fast. I need my family home and safe before it hits.

As the thought crosses my mind, I pause, realizing something that hits me harder than expected—when I thought of my family, I was including Willow. The weight of that realization sinks in, making me sigh. By the end of the day, who knows if she'll still be in my life? She could be drafting her resignation letter right now, and after what she saw, I wouldn't blame her.

I push the thought aside for now and head back inside, making my way to the basement. I step into the garage and immediately notice Sal's car is gone.

What the hell happened?

My eyes scan the area, trying to piece it together. Sal wouldn't just leave without a word, not without checking in with me first. Something's not right, and my gut twists with the possibilities. I move further into the garage, the cold creeping into my bones as I assess the situation.

I hurry down the stairs into the basement, my pulse quickening as I approach the hallway. The door to the interrogation room is open, and immediately, I know something's gone wrong. I can feel it in the air, a sickening sense that something's spiraled out of control.

"Boss!" Sal l's voice calls out., strained but urgent.

I rush into the room and see him slumped against the wall; a nasty wound slashed across his face. Blood drips down his cheek, but there's no sign of Jack. My gut twists with anger and frustration as I rush to Sal's side.

"What the hell happened?" I demand, my voice sharp as I check the wound. It's deep but not life-threatening.

Sal waves me off, grimacing. "I'm fine, boss. Jack must've taken advantage of the confusion with Willow to loosen his bindings. He caught me off guard—hit me hard, cut me with the bone saw, and then took my keys in the chaos."

I let out a loud, furious "*Shit!*" that echoes through the room. The situation has gone from bad to worse, and now we've got a loose end on the run.

"You need to get that cut looked at," I tell Sal.

Sal shakes his head. , stubborn as ever. "I'm fine, boss. I owe it to you to find Jack ASAP."

I nod, knowing he's right, but still uneasy. "I need to go check on Lucia. We'll regroup after. Take one of my cars and go."

Sal nods, holding a handkerchief to his face, and I turn on my heel, my mind shifting back to the girls and Willow.

This day is far from over, and it's about to get a hell of a lot worse if we don't get this situation under control.

CHAPTER 23

WILLOW

Nico showed up just a little after us., looking like he was carrying the weight of the world on his shoulders. He barely said a word, except to his little girls, making sure they were okay. It was sweet, but also kind of eerie—like there was this whole other side of him he was keeping under wraps. I guess after what I saw in the basement, I shouldn't be surprised.

The doctor put butterfly stitches over the small cut and reassured us that Lucia didn't have a concussion. We all breathed a sigh of relief.

Now, we're in Ms. M's car, heading back to Nico's place. The snow's coming down hard, making the roads slick. Nico's in his car, driving with the girls, and my thoughts are all over the place.

I don't even know what I want to do. Part of me wants to get as far away from this whole situation as possible—just pack up and leave. But then there's the other part, the part that's still stuck on how Nico was with his girls, how he was with me before everything went sideways. It's confusing as hell, and I'm not sure which way I'm leaning.

Also, I'm carrying the man's child. That adds a whole other level to this convoluted mess I've found myself in.

The car's quiet, except for the soft hum of the heater and the sound of snow hitting the windows. I can't shake the feeling that something big is coming, and I have no idea if I'm ready for it.

We pull up to the house, and part of me doesn't want to get out of the car. Ms. M sighs beside me, like there's something heavy on her mind.

She breaks the silence first. "I know what you're thinking," she says, her voice gentle but firm. "But believe it or not, Mr. Conti is a good man. He just comes from a certain tradition, one that surely seems strange to people who didn't grow up the way he did."

I can't help but laugh, but it's a dry, hollow sound. "A tradition?"

Ms. M chuckles a little, though it's tinged with something like nostalgia. "That's the term my parents used when they explained it to me."

I raise an eyebrow, giving her a sideways look. "So, you come from this sort of lifestyle too?"

She nods, and it's like a piece of the puzzle clicks into place. No wonder she's so calm, so in control, even when things go sideways. She's been in this world longer than I have.

I shake my head, letting out a breath I didn't realize I was holding. "What the heck have I gotten myself into?"

Ms. M just gives me a knowing smile but doesn't say anything else. And honestly, what more is there to say? I'm in deep, and there's no easy way out.

We pull into the garage, and I can feel my whole body tense up. My eyes automatically drift to the door that leads to the basement. There's no movement, no sign of activity, but I wonder. Is that guy still in there, still bleeding out? Does he still have all his fingers?

"Don't think about it," Ms. M says, her voice cutting through my thoughts like she's reading my mind.

We park, and I shake off the thoughts as best as I can. I get out and help get the girls from Nico's backseat. They both look as exhausted as I feel after the whole ordeal.

When we step into the kitchen, I glance at the clock and see that it's already 4:30. The girls have long missed their naps, and it's no wonder they look so sleepy.

Ms. M notices too and suggests, "Maybe an early dinner and bedtime would be best."

"Yeah, that sounds good," I agree, still feeling a bit off-kilter.

Nico walks in with Lucia in his arms, and she's already half-asleep. The tension eases a bit—thankfully, the injury wasn't as bad as we feared.

"I'm going to give her a bath and feed her upstairs," Nico says, his voice softer than usual. He glances at me, and for a second, there's this look—like he's wondering if this is the last time he'll see me. It hits me, but before I can even process it, he's already heading upstairs with Lucia.

I glance out the window. The snow's really coming down. No way I'm leaving tonight, even if I wanted to. Looks like the storm's making that decision for me.

Ms. M must see the look on my face because she steps in with a reassuring smile. "Why don't you sit down? I'll whip up something to eat. Just relax."

I nod, too drained to argue, and collapse into a chair at the kitchen table. My mind's a mess, but I focus on Ms. M as she moves around the kitchen like a pro. In no time, she's whipped up a creamy mushroom risotto that smells amazing. She hands a plate to Giulia, who dives right in, and then sets one in front of me.

"Eat up."

I ," she says with a knowing smile. I take a bite, and for a moment, it's like the world isn't crashing down around me.

I take one more bite, then another, and before I even realize it, my plate is clean. The food's so good, I don't even care that I practically inhaled it. Without saying a word, Ms. M. scoops another serving onto my plate, and I just keep eating, my eyes fixed on the snow swirling outside.

Eventually, Giulia pipes up, "Can I be excused to watch TV?"

Ms. M smiles at her. "If you get into your pajamas all by yourself, then yes, you can watch a little TV before bed."

Giulia's face lights up, and she bolts out of the kitchen, clearly thrilled with the deal. I keep eating until I'm finally, blissfully full, then lean back in my chair, feeling a little more human.

Ms. M watches me with a satisfied smile. "How was it?"

"Amazing. ," I say, patting my stomach. "Exactly what I needed."

"There's cannoli in the fridge." Her eye twinkles a little after she speaks.

I laugh, shaking my head.I laugh "I seriously couldn't eat another bite."

Ms. M. leans in with a playful wink. "You know, Italian women take words like that as a challenge."

I can't help but grin. "Well, I'm not about to get in the way of tradition, but I'm waving the white flag this time."

Without another word, Ms. M. opens the fridge and pulls out the cannolis. She grabs two plates, places a cannoli on each, and sits down next to me, sliding one over.

I glance at it and ask, "Can I get a fork?"

Ms. M. laughs, shaking her head. "You don't eat cannoli with a fork. You eat it like this." She picks hers up and takes a huge bite, not caring about the powdered sugar dusting her lips.

I raise an eyebrow but follow suit, taking a big bite, and wow —it's as delicious as it looks. We eat in comfortable silence for a minute, the kitchen filled with the sounds of chewing and the occasional contented sigh.

Eventually, I ask, "Why are you being so nice to me? I clearly defied you earlier."

Ms. M smiles. "Let's just say I understand more than you think. You've been through a lot today, more than most would handle. Doesn't hurt to show a little kindness, right?"

I nod, appreciating the moment. "Yeah, I guess you're right."

Ms. M wipes her hands on a napkin and looks at me with a knowing smile. "There's something else," she says. , her tone casual but serious. "You're damn good at your job, Willow."

I nearly choke on my cannoli, coughing as I laugh. "You really think so?"

"I do," Ms. M. says, nodding. "Kids bump their heads—it's practically a hobby for them. But you stayed calm under pressure, handled the situation, and did what needed to be done. That's what matters."

I blink, a little thrown by the compliment.

"And then," Ms. M. continues, leaning in slightly, "there's the little matter of what you saw downstairs."

I freeze, my stomach doing a flip. "Yeah, about that..."

"Like it or not," she says , her voice steady but firm, "you're part of our world now. You know more than most people should, and you've proven you can handle it."

I don't know how to feel about that. Part of me wants to scream, "Get me the hell out of here!" But another part— the part that's still sitting at this table, eating cannoli and feeling almost... comfortable—makes me pause.

I push my plate aside, suddenly not so hungry. "I didn't exactly ask for this, you know."

"No one ever does." Ms. M leans back in her chair, her eyes soft but serious. "Some people are born into this life, like me and Mr. Conti. And some are pulled into it, like you."

I don't say anything, but her words hit harder than I expected. I've felt like that for a while now, like I've been getting closer and closer to something I couldn't turn away from. Seeing what happened downstairs today? That was just a formality. Something I knew was coming, even if I didn't want to admit it.

"I guess I could've walked out the door at any time," I say quietly, more to myself than to Ms. M.

She nods. "You still can. It's not too late. Mr. Conti would be disappointed, but he'd understand."

I glance out the window, watching the snow fall in thick, heavy flakes. The world outside looks so peaceful, so untouched by everything swirling around me. But I know it's not just the snow keeping me here.

I could leave, but something keeps pulling me back. The girls. I've come to love them. And Nico, and the fact that I'm pregnant with his child.

I turn back to Ms. M, my curiosity getting the best of me. "What happened to Mrs. Conti?"

She pauses, her expression shifting just slightly. She corrects me, her voice firm. "There is no Mrs. Conti."

I blink, confused.I'm confused. "So, what, the girls just got dropped off by a stork or something?"

Ms. M gives a small smile, but then says something that makes me pause. . "The truth isn't too far off from that."

I lean in, curious.

She leans back in her chair, her gaze distant, like she's pulling the memory from the past. "It was a cool summer night, four years ago. Out of nowhere, there was a knock at the door. When I opened it, I found two car seats and those two little beauties upstairs. There was a note tucked inside one of the seats that read, 'I can't do it. Please, take care of them.'"

I am stunned as she continues.

"I brought the girls in and immediately called Mr. Conti. The moment he saw them, I could tell he knew exactly what had happened. He'd had a brief fling with a woman nearly a year prior, and she couldn't raise them, so she left them at his door."

I raise an eyebrow, still processing. "Was he hesitant to take them in?"

Ms. M shakes her head, a soft smile on her face. "Not even for a second. The moment he saw them, he fell in love. From that night on, they were his world."

Ms. M's smile falters a bit as she continues. "A new part of Mr. Conti was born that day, just as surely as those little girls were brought into this world—a side of him that's loving, protective, and fiercely devoted." She pauses, giving me a pointed look. "And I get the sense he's ready to bring you into that part of his world."

I tense, her words hitting a little too close to home. Does she know? No way, I think, trying to shake it off. But there's something about the way she looks at me that makes me feel like she knows more than she's letting on.

She stands up. , her calm presence filling the room. "I'll put the girls to bed. I imagine you've got quite a bit to talk about with Mr. Conti."

I glance at her, my mind spinning, but all I can manage is a quiet, "Thank you, Ms. M. Seriously."

She smiles warmly, her usual professional demeanor softening. She smiles. "Call me Olivia."

With that, she walks off, leaving me sitting there with a lot more questions than answers.

CHAPTER 24

WILLOW

I'm alone again, and as soon as the silence wraps around me, that damn scene from the basement crashes back into my mind. I can see it so clearly—the man tied up, blood trickling down, Nico standing next to him with that awful tool, ready to make him suffer more. The memory makes my stomach churn, the bile rising in my throat.

It's not just the violence, it's the contrast that's tearing me up inside.

How can Nico, the same man who's so tender with his girls, so loving and gentle with me, be capable of something so dark? The question gnaws at me. Who *is* this man?

I look down, placing my hand on my belly, and the weight of it hits me all over again. Whatever darkness is inside of him, it's a part of me now, too. Part of the baby growing inside me. The thought makes my chest tighten, the anxiety swirling in my head.

What am I supposed to do? I'm trapped between two versions of Nico—the loving father and lover, and the man capable of unspeakable things.

I don't have answers, but I know one thing for sure: this choice I have to make is going to change everything.

I watch the snow falling harder, piling up outside. With each inch that builds, the chances of me leaving slip away. But if I'm being real, it's not just the snow keeping me here.

Olivia's words keep bouncing around in my head: women like us are drawn to this life. Is that actually true? Is there some part of me that finds Nico's dark side... *appealing*? The thought sends a weird rush through me, one I can't totally shake.

Before I can untangle it, I hear heavy footsteps coming down the hallway. My heart skips a beat, and I don't even need to look to know it's Nico. He's coming, and I have no idea what I'm going to say.

He steps into the kitchen, and immediately, there's something different about him. He's always been huge—built like a damn tank—but right now, he feels even bigger, more imposing.

More dangerous.

Maybe it's because now I know who he is, what he's capable of.

I clear my throat, trying to shake off the feeling. "How are the girls?"

He steps closer, his presence dominating the room. "Both sleeping soundly," he says, his voice low and rich, like it's wrapping around me, pulling me in.

Even his voice is a weapon. It hits me like a warm blanket, melting whatever resistance I thought I had left.

I want him. There's no denying it. My brain's screaming at me to run, but my body? My body's already made the decision to stay.

Nico moves closer, standing over me, and suddenly the room feels smaller—like the only thing that exists is him. It's so quiet, I swear I can hear the soft whisper of snow falling outside, but inside, my heart is pounding. My body's buzzing, every nerve alive, and I know he can sense it. I'm practically radiating need, and it's only getting stronger with every second.

Finally, I take a deep breath.h, my voice shaky as I ask, "Can you take me to my room?"

He smirks, just a hint of it curling his lips.. "I give the orders, remember?" he says, his voice low and commanding. "You come to *my* room."

My throat dries up, and all I can do is nod, unable to form another word. He grabs my hand, pulling me gently along behind him, and the contact alone sends a shiver down my spine. .

He leads me out of the kitchen, up the stairs, and I follow without question, feeling like I'm being driven by pure, animal need. Every step, every glance back from him, only makes me want him more.

I stop dead when we get to his room—a fire crackling in the fireplace, filling the space with a warm, cozy glow. Did he plan this? Like he knew I'd end up here, like he knew I'd want him?

"You're bold."

He smirks, totally unfazed. "I know."

He shuts the door behind us, and the soft *click* sends a jolt of heat through me. He moves to the edge of the bed, sitting down, and I swear his eyes on me feel heavier than they should. Like he's undressing me with that stare alone.

His gaze sweeps over me, slow and deliberate, making me feel like I'm the only thing in the room that matters.

"Take off your clothes. s," he says, his voice low and commanding. "Slowly."

My breath hitches, but tThere's no hesitation. I start peeling off my clothes, doing exactly what he wants, all while feeling his eyes roam over me like they're touching my skin. By the time I'm down to just my bra and panties, I can barely think straight. My whole body's on fire, humming with this need that's all too real.

"Come here," he says, his tone leaving zero room for debate.."

I make my way over to him, purposely swaying my hips a little more than usual, knowing he's watching my every move. I can practically feel his eyes eating me up. The tension is thick, electric, and by the time I reach him, I'm already soaking wet.

He grabs me by the hips and pulls me close, the sudden contact sending a jolt of excitement through me. I can feel his hardness pressing against me through his pants, and it takes everything in me not to let out a shaky breath..

"What are you thinking?" he asks, his voice low and teasing, like he already knows the answer but wants to hear me say it.

I bite my lip, feeling the tension build even more. "It turns me on to know I make you so hard.",", I finally say, my voice barely above a whisper.

His eyes darken, that smirk of his returning. "I want to see how turned on *you* are."

I blink, my pulse quickening. "Oh, I'm *very* turned on."

"Lay on the bed," he orders. As I lay down, he gets up, walking over to the chair beside the bed and sitting down, watching me like a predator ready to pounce. "Take off your panties," he commands, his voice deep and steady.

I slide my panties off, feeling the cool air hit me as I toss them aside. His eyes roam over me, taking in every inch. "You're so fucking sexy," he says, and I smile slowly at him.

But then his voice drops even lower. "Touch yourself."

I hesitate, feeling a little embarrassed. But just like before, this isn't a suggestion—it's an order. Slowly, I let my hand slide down between my legs, the heat of my own touch mixing with the intensity of his gaze.

And just like that, I'm lost in the moment.

I start touching myself, fingers slipping between my legs, slow at first. My breathing hitches as I get into a rhythm, dipping my fingers inside myself to gather my juices and then circling my clit, building the tension inside me.

Nico watches me, his eyes burning with the intensity that always drives me crazy.with desire.

"Close your eyes," he murmurs, his voice low and dripping with heat.. "Let whatever comes to mind take over."

I do as he says, letting the darkness behind my eyelids pull me in. My thoughts immediately flash to him taking me in all sorts of ways, the roughness, the passion, the way he always knows exactly what I need. My fingers move faster, the pleasure building.

He must sense it, because he leans in, his voice rough but seductive. "Come for me."

And that's all it takes. My body arches, and I fall over the edge, shuddering as the orgasm rips through me, wave after wave of pleasure leaving me breathless.

I take one deep breath, then another, trying to ground myself after what just happened. I can't believe how hard I made myself come. As I'm still catching my breath, Nico rises from his chair and pulls off his shirt, revealing his chiseled body. My mouth practically waters at the sight of him.

His eyes drift down, and I notice them lingering on my belly for just a second. My heart skips a beat. Does he know? There's no way—I'm too early to be showing. But it's like he can sense it somehow, and the thought makes my pulse race even faster.

He steps closer, his voice impossibly deep and full of raw, dangerous energy. "I'm going to take you," he growls, his eyes burning into mine. "Claim you. Make you mine. All mine."

I'm practically soaking the sheets below me, ready for him.

"Are you ready?" he asks.

"So ready," I whisper, feeling the heat build between us all over again.."

At this moment, there's no hesitation.

I'm completely his.

She's laying on my bed, sprawled out like a goddess, the sexiest goddamn thing I've ever seen. Her skin's still flushed from her orgasm, her pussy glistening, and the way she's looking at me is different from before.

I can tell the scene in the basement's still fresh on her mind, but right now, none of that matters.

She's mine at this moment, completely, and she knows it. She wants it.

She's waiting, her eyes on me, her body tense with anticipation. She wants me to take control, to tell her what to do.

And I will.

"Give me your hand."

She doesn't hesitate, lifting her hand toward me, and I grip it firmly, pulling her off the bed with ease. Before she can catch her breath, I've got her in my arms, her soft body pressed against mine. My cock is hard, aching, and I press it against her pussy, watching the way her breath catches as she feels it.

Her eyes flicker up to mine, wide and ready, waiting for my next move, waiting for me to take what's mine. I grab her by the ass, lifting her like she weighs nothing. Her legs wrap around me instinctively, and I press my mouth onto hers, kissing her hard.

She kisses me back just as fiercely, her tongue desperate, as if she's trying to devour me..

"Take hold of me. ," I pull back and order, my voice thick with desire. "Guide my cock inside you."

Without hesitation, her hand slips between us, fingers wrapping perfectly around my shaft. She guides me in, the tight heat of her pussy enveloping me inch by inch. Her grip is firm, perfect—just like every other time—but this moment feels different. She's giving herself to me fully, and the sensation of bottoming out inside her is intoxicating.

She buries her face into my shoulder, her breath hot against my skin. I hold her there for a second, savoring the feeling of being buried so deep inside her. There's no rush. She's mine, and I'm going to take my time making sure she never forgets it.

I fuck her like this, her legs wrapped tightly around my waist as I bounce her on my cock. Her hair's flying wild, her breasts bouncing with every thrust. She's completely in my control, just the way I like it.

Her body responds to me with every move, and I can feel how close she is, how much she's holding on. "Let go," I growl, my voice low and rough. "Give yourself to me. I've got you."

I'm driving up into her, deeper and harder with each thrust, and I can see it—her eyes rolling back, her mouth open, gasping for air. She's lost in it, in me. The heat between us is building, pushing her closer to the edge.

"Come for me."

She grips me tightly, her body shuddering as she falls over the edge, her orgasm hitting hard. Her juices drip down my cock, soaking me as she clings to me, her nails digging into my shoulders.

I hold her tightly, savoring the feeling of her coming undone in my arms, knowing she's all mine. Every moan, every tremble, it's all for me.

I lay her on the bed, her breasts rising and falling with each ragged breath. The sight of her—completely lost in the frenzy of what we just did—fuels something primal in me. She's still flushed, her body trembling slightly, and I drink it all in like it's life-saving water.

I climb onto the bed, my body pressing down with intent. I flip her over, her perfect, heart-shaped ass now on full display, her pussy glistening with arousal. It's all too tempting.

I position myself over her and plunge in, taking her from behind with no hesitation. She lets out a gasp, and I push deeper, Willow lying flat on her stomach beneath me, her ass raised just enough for me to drive down hard and deep, over and over again.

I reach down and give her a firm smack on the ass, watching as the red mark forms on her soft skin. Her moan is all the confirmation I need that she's loving every second of it. I land another smack, and she pushes back against me, feeding off the roughness.

"How does it feel?" I growl, my voice rough with need.

"It's... fucking... incredible."

Her words light a fire inside me, and I thrust harder, driving deeper into her, knowing she's right there with me.

I'm ready to finish with her.

I flip Willow over, grabbing her ankles and spreading her legs wide. The perfect angle. She squirms toward me, her body practically begging for me to be back inside her. Her desperation is intense, and it only fuels me more.

I lean down, my lips brushing her ear as I growl, "I'm going to make you come harder than you ever have, and when you do, you'll be mine. Only mine. Understand?"

She nods, eyes wide, barely able to contain herself.

I sit up, throw her legs over my shoulders, and drive into her hard. Her back arches, her mouth open in a silent moan, her body shaking as I pound into her. The sight of her underneath me, completely taken by the pleasure, is intoxicating.

Her breasts bounce with every thrust, her skin flushed and glistening with sweat. She's a mess of want and need, her hands gripping the sheets like she's holding on for dear life.

I thrust deeper, faster, feeling her tighten around me. She's close, and so am I. The pressure builds inside me, each stroke pushing me closer to the edge. I can feel her body quivering beneath me, every muscle tensing as her orgasm approaches. I reach between us and circle my thumb over her swollen clit and feel her instantly clench around my cock.

"Come Willow. Now," I growl, feeling my own release building, ready to let go.

She comes hard, her entire body tightening around me as she grabs me tight, her moans filling the room. It's enough to push me over the edge, and I finish with her, releasing deep inside, my body shuddering with the force of it. I grunt, holding her in place, making sure she takes every last drop.

The moment hangs in the air, heavy and electric, as our breathing slowly begins to steady.

When we're done, I slide out of her and pull her into my arms, pressing her against my chest. I cover her face with kisses, her skin still hot from the intensity of what we just shared.

"How do you feel?" I ask, my voice low, still a little rough from the release.

She catches her breath, smiling up at me, her face flushed. "Like nothing I've ever felt before."

I grin, satisfied. "Good. ," I say, my voice dropping an octave as I brush a strand of hair from her face. "Because this is just the beginning."

She leans into me, and for a moment, the world feels still. But in the back of my mind, I know we're only scratching the surface of what's between us—there's so much more to come, and I'm finally ready to claim it all.

CHAPTER 26

WILLOW

My eyes are locked on the wounds on Nico's shoulder, where I dug my nails into his skin earlier.

He's fast asleep next to me, his powerful chest rising and falling with each breath. But I can't stop staring at the marks I left on him.

The sight of blood doesn't freak me out like it should.

It's kind of ironic, honestly. One minute, I'm watching Nico draw blood from another man, and not long after, I'm drawing blood from *him*. It's completely different, but the blood is there, nonetheless. The thought hits me hard—if I'm going to be in Nico's world, blood might just become part of the routine.

That's a lot to take in.

I'm still in a daze from the sex. God, it was intense. Aggressive. It was everything I didn't even know I'd been wanting, but now that I've had a taste, I'm hooked.

Every part of me is still buzzing, and I can't help but wonder how I got here. One second, I'm walking into a normal life, and the next? I'm tangled up with a man who's as dangerous as he is irresistible.

Nico stirs a little, his arm moving to rest on me, and I feel a warmth bloom in my chest. I know I should be freaked out, but I'm not. Despite all the danger and darkness, Nico makes me feel safe.

I get up quietly, leaving him sleeping, and walk over to the glass door that overlooks the balcony and the backyard garden beyond. The snow's really coming down now, thick and relentless, coating everything in a soft, white blanket. I sigh, pressing my forehead against the cool glass, thinking about the mess I've walked into.

Just a few hours ago, I was almost certain I'd leave. Get out before things get too deep. But all it took was one hard look from Nico, and I'd melted like putty in his hands, turning into his willing little toy.

The craziest part? I don't regret a damn thing about it.

But now, standing here, I wonder if I should be embarrassed by how easily I gave in. This man is dangerous. I've seen it with my own eyes. And yet, in bed, that danger felt... intoxicating. Like I craved it. I almost hate myself for how much I loved it.

His life is a weird balancing act—maintaining the line between being the caring father and partner and whatever the hell he is when he's not at home. But what happens if that line blurs? Or worse—breaks?

I place my hand on my belly, something I've been doing a lot since I found out I'm pregnant. The weight of it hits me as I turn to look at Nico, still asleep, his chest rising and falling steadily. This isn't just the man I've fallen for—this is the father of my child.

And he's a mobster. No doubt about it now.

Before, I could pretend, make excuses, tell myself he wasn't really associated with the mob. That whatever shady business he was into wasn't that serious. But after what I saw today? All those delusions were blown to pieces. He's in deep. And now, so am I.

But Nico's more than his job. Yeah, he lives a dangerous life, but I've fallen for him. Hard. And in such a short time, too. It's wild. I barely know him, yet somehow, I *do*. I know the way he looks at his girls, the way he's tender with me even after being this lethal force of nature. I've seen both sides of him, and even though I should probably run, I don't want to.

I yawn, feeling the weight of the day hit me all at once. I'm ready to crash. I wander over to the dresser, looking for something to sleep in. After rummaging through a few drawers, I find one with T-shirts, all perfectly folded. I grab one and pull it on. It's huge on me, practically swallowing me up, but it smells like him, and it's comforting in a way I can't really explain.

Something catches my eye, and I push back the stack of T-shirts, and my heart skips when I see what's hidden underneath—a thick stack of cash and a gun. The gun's attached to the drawer, locked up tight, definitely not for casual use. There's no way anyone but Nico has access to it.

I stare at it for a second. How many other stashes like this are hidden around the house? It's wild, but it's also reality now.

This is my world.

I close the drawer quietly, like I didn't just stumble upon another piece of Nico's dangerous life. Slipping back into bed, I feel his strong arm wrap around me, pulling me close. Despite everything, despite all the questions and the chaos, a smile sneaks its way onto my lips.

I wake up to a loud banging on the door, groggy as hell. Sunlight's pouring into the room, and for a second, I can't even process what's happening. Before I can react, Nico's out of bed and rushing to the door. He swings it open, and there they are: the girls. They burst into the room, full of energy, chattering nonstop about the snow and how they have to get outside and play in it.

I pull the covers up a little higher. Have they seen me? They're so excited about the snow, maybe they're too distracted to care.

Surprisingly, for all his previous warnings about this very possibility, Nico seems totally unbothered. He ruffles the girls' hair, asking them how much snow they think they've got to play with.

The girls are bouncing around like they've had ten cups of coffee.

"Papa, can we have pancakes for breakfast? Pleeease!" Lucia practically begs, her eyes wide and impossible to say no to..

Nico chuckles, getting down to their level. "Pancakes, huh? What about some eggs? You need protein if you're gonna play in all that snow."

Giulia jumps in., , her excitement almost vibrating off her. "Yeah, eggs too!"

Lucia nods like her life depends on it. "Yeah! And we *have* to build the biggest snowman ever!"

Nico grins. , playing right into their energy. "Alright, alright. Pancakes and eggs it is. After breakfast, we'll build the biggest snowman this neighborhood's ever seen."

Just when I think the girls haven't noticed me and I'm in the clear, Giulia's eyes land on me. She stares for a second before asking, "Why are you in Papa's room?"

Cue the panic. But of course, Nico's smooth as hell. Doesn't even blink. "Oh, we were having a little secret chat about Christmas presents," he says, winking like it's no big deal. "Had to keep it quiet so you two wouldn't hear."

The girls giggle, totally buying it. "Ooooh, presents!" Giulia claps her hands, and then they're off, running out of the room.

I let out a breath, scrambling to get dressed. As I'm pulling on my clothes, Nico grabs me by the waist and pulls me in for a kiss.

"I'll be out in a few minutes," he says, all smirks and confidence.."

I can't wait.

CHAPTER 27

NICO

I'm seated at *Il Vecchio's*, one of the many businesses my family owns. The place is shut down for the day—snowstorm's got half the city on pause.

But snow doesn't stop my work. It never does.

Sal steps out from the back, wiping his hands on a towel. "Everyone's here," he says.

I nod, taking a slow sip of wine. This meeting's been weighing heavily on my mind. I know the stakes—this could tip everything into war. But I'm not worried. War doesn't scare me; I've been trained for it; I've planned for it.

I stand, adjusting my suit jacket. With a glance at Sal, I head to the back meeting room.

Inside, fifteen men wait, their eyes locking on me the second I walk in. These aren't just any men—they're my lieutenants. The ones who execute my orders, handle my operations, and keep everything running smoothly. Through them, I control the empire. The restaurants, the clubs, the streets—they all answer to me through these men.

I take my time, making eye contact with each one of them. They're all waiting for me to speak, to lead them.

I walk to the head of the table and take my place.

One of the lieutenants steps up and refills my wine. I take the glass, my eyes moving from face to face, reading each of them. Some are calm, others are trying to hide what's really going on inside. I can feel the weight of what's unsaid in the room.

I clear my throat and break the silence. "There are more than a few empty seats here today," I start, my voice steady. "Men who were killed alongside my father."

The room is still, no one daring to move. I let my gaze drift across the table. "And as I look around at the faces of my inner circle, my father's inner circle, I can sense the tension. Maybe even some mistrust. Some of you might think you should be sitting in my chair right now. Running this empire. But let me make this clear—it's *not* up for debate."

My words cut through the room, the air thick with unspoken thoughts.. "I'm the boss, just as my father intended," I continue, my tone harder now. "And I expect every one of you to fall in line. You don't have to like me, but you will respect me."

I pause, letting that sink in. "I might be new to my father's seat, but I'm not new to this game. Anyone who thinks they can cross me, try their hand at taking control? Do so at your own peril."

Silence. They understand what's being said.

I lean back in my chair, my gaze steady as I address the room. "I assume Sal filled you in on the current situation. We're doing everything we can to get to the bottom of who attacked the Conti family."

Paolo Di Luca, one of my more seasoned lieutenants, speaks up. "It sounds like someone who knows something is on the run?"

I nod, my eyes locking on his. "That's right. A man going by the name Jack. Then again, that might not even be his real name. Says he's a money guy for the Rossis, but something doesn't add up." I pause, letting the weight of my words hang in the air. "But he's the closest thing we've got to a lead."

Before I can continue, Angelo Rosetti speaks up, his voice dripping with frustration. "We don't need leads, boss. Let's call it what it is—the Rossis are behind the hit. Everyone knows it."

A murmur ripples through the room, and I catch a few nods from the other men. I narrow my eyes but keep my tone calm, controlled.

"You think I don't know the Rossis are involved? Of course they've got their hands in this. But we're not making any moves until we have every piece of the puzzle. I don't do guesswork. We're not going to act on assumptions and chase shadows."

Angelo quiets down, but I lean forward. , making sure my next words hit hard. "We'll strike when I say so. Not a second before. Do you all understand?"

The room falls into silence. They know exactly who's calling the shots here..

"The top priority for all Conti operations right now is to find this prick, Jack. I don't care how long it takes or where he's hiding—we *will* get to the bottom of who the fuck killed my father and our men. And understand this: the life of anyone who stands in my way is forfeit. Even if they're sitting in this room."

The tension rises, but no one says a word. I ask again, my voice like steel. "Am I understood?"

There's a chorus of nods and murmured agreements.

Paolo speaks up again, his voice cautious but steady. "We could use some of our contacts at the docks, shake a few trees down there. If Jack's trying to disappear, he might look for a way out of the city by boat."

Angelo, calmer now, adds, "I've got some connections in the clubs. Jack's not a ghost. If he's spending money, we'll know."

"Good," I nod, appreciating the initiative. "Do it. Both of you. I want updates by the end of the week."

Another lieutenant, Franco Moretti, speaks up. "We could hit up our street-level dealers. They hear everything. Junkies aren't exactly known for their discretion."

"Smart move," I say. "Get on it."

I dismiss the room, my gaze hard as the men file out. "Sal," I say, holding him back. We've got more to discuss.

Sal starts off, apologetic. "I'm sorry again, boss, for letting Jack get the drop on me."

NANNY FOR THE DON | 199

I wave him off. "One fuck-up isn't gonna ruin your reputation with me, Sal. Let it go."

I lean in, lowering my voice. "You could sense it in the room, right?"

Sal nods, his expression darkening. "War."

"That's right," I say. "Half the lieutenants in there walked out pissed because I didn't give the green light. They're itching for it."

Sal leans back, crossing his arms. "Makes sense. The Rossis have been a pain in our ass for years. They want to end it."

"Not to mention," I continue, "war's a chance for lieutenants to make their names. Get in good with the new boss."

Sal smirks, nodding. "Ambition."

"Or r," I add, locking eyes with him, "a chance to take out the new boss."

He falls silent for a moment. Then he nods slowly, understanding exactly what I'm saying. We both know the truth—when you're in a seat of power, everyone's got an angle. Some are loyal, but others? They're just waiting for their shot.

Sal leans back, his eyes on me. "You're the man in charge, boss. Whatever you say, goes."

I raise an eyebrow. "But..."

"But," Sal continues, "war might be on the horizon. There *is* a damn good chance the Rossis were behind the hit. If that's true..."

I nod, cutting him off. "If that's true, then we handle it. But I'm not jumping into all out bloodshed because a few lieutenants are itching to prove themselves."

Sal nods, respecting the decision. "Still, we need to be ready."

"Exactly. y," I reply. "I won't let them pressure me into anything, but we're not going in blind either. We'll have a battle plan in place, just in case."

Sal's eyes narrow. "That means we need another meeting. One where we lay out what each lieutenant's gonna be responsible for when things go south."

"I agree. But not here, not in the city. We need somewhere outside of town. No prying eyes. No ears listening in."

Sal nods, understanding the need for discretion.

"I've got a place in mind," I say, leaning forward. "One of our old warehouses in Yonkers."

Sal smirks, nodding. "Perfect spot. Quiet, out of the way, and no one's gonna poke their nose where it doesn't belong."

I nod, but my tone hardens. "And I don't want any more business being handled at my home. Not after what happened last time."

Sal nods in agreement. "If I find Jack, I'll keep him on ice. Won't bring him near your place, I promise."

"Good," I say, standing up. "Let the lieutenants know what's on the docket. The meeting's happening tomorrow. I'll be in touch with the time, but I want everyone ready."

Sal nods again, pulling out his phone. "I'll take care of it."

"And Sal," I add, my voice firm, "I'll be spending the night at the warehouse. I want eyes on the place to make sure we're secure."

"Got it, boss."

As I turn to leave, the gravity of what's coming settles in. We're not at war yet, but the pieces are in motion. It's only a matter of time.

I grab my glass of wine and sit at the empty bar, the events of the last few days playing on a loop in my head. There's no escaping it—until my father's killer is brought down, none of us are safe. Not me, not Willow, and definitely not my daughters.

The thought of something happening to any of them makes my blood run hot, rage boiling just beneath the surface. I take a long sip of wine, forcing myself to calm down. Losing my cool won't get us anywhere.

I pull out my phone, ready to text Willow. I'll let her know I'll be away on business for the night, to keep an eye on the girls. The fact that I trust her to look after them gives me some peace. She's become a part of my life now, whether I planned it or not.

And with that comes responsibility. Her safety is on me. She might not fully understand the world she's stepped into, but I do.

I type out the message, keeping it short. *I'll be home in a bit. Something came up. We'll discuss.*

As I hit send, the weight of it all sinks in. I've got enemies circling, but as long as I'm breathing, I'll make damn sure nothing touches Willow or the kids.

Willow texts back almost immediately. *Is everything alright?*

I look at the screen, the words staring back at me. *For now, yes*, I respond. *We'll talk when I get home.*

After I send it, I think about how the hell I'm going to pull her deeper into this world without breaking her. She deserves to know the risks, the real danger she's in just being around me. But at the same time, I can't afford to scare her off—not now, not when things are this close to boiling over.

Tomorrow's meeting with the lieutenants will be crucial. We'll iron out the battle plan, prepare for whatever's coming. If I need to, I'll send Willow, Olivia, and the girls out of town—somewhere far from the bloodshed that's about to rain down.

CHAPTER 28

WILLOW

I'm sitting at home, the girls finally down for their afternoon nap, but I'm a mess of nerves.

Olivia's out getting groceries, so I'm here by myself, no one to talk to, and this uneasy feeling just won't go away. I can't shake the thought that Nico isn't telling me something. Something big.

I'm glad he's on his way back. Hopefully, I won't be in the dark much longer.

I hear the chime—the one that means his car just pulled in. My heart does this little flip, and I feel this crazy rush of excitement. I swear, I'm like a teenager again, all giddy at the idea of seeing him. Which is ridiculous, because falling for a mobster? Probably the worst idea I've ever had.

And yet... I think I'm in love. God help me.

The door to the garage opens, and there he is, stepping into the kitchen. His presence fills the room, and my heart practically melts on the spot. He's got that look on his face that makes me weak in the knees.

I try to play it cool, but it's useless. I'm completely wrapped up in him, whether I want to admit it or not. This might be love, as ill-advised as it is.

I can't help it. The second I see him, I rush over and throw my arms around him. His hands immediately go to my face, pulling me in for a kiss, and I melt into it, completely lost in him. The second his lips leave mine; a wave of sadness hits me like a ton of bricks. Oh shit. I'm in deep. Way deeper than I ever expected.

He pulls back slightly and looks at me. "Sit," he says, and I know it's not a suggestion. I do as he says, my mind spinning. "I'll be out of town for work overnight," he tells me, his tone steady. "Ms. M will be here if you need anything."

Curiosity buzzes at the back of my mind, but all that comes out is, "Will you be safe?"

He pulls me in for a tight hug, his chin resting on the top of my head. "I'll be fine," he murmurs, his voice calm but firm.

I wish I knew more, but he doesn't offer details. And I don't push. We both know how this works.

Before I can dwell on it, he kisses me again, deeper this time. My heart does this stupid little flip, and I am wrapped up in the moment. When he pulls away, we share this intense moment of eye contact. It's like there's so much between us that neither of us are saying out loud, but we both feel it.

Feelings. So many damn feelings.

I almost slip and tell him I'm pregnant.

The words are right there, about to fall out of my mouth, but I stop myself just in time. Now's not the moment. He's got too much going on, too much weighing on him, and the last thing he needs is something else to worry about.

He catches my hesitation and raises an eyebrow. "What's on your mind?"

I panic for a second, then quickly say, "Just... thinking about what to get you for Christmas."

His smile is instant, and he pulls me in for another kiss. I smile against his lips, my nerves easing just a bit.

"How are the girls?" he asks as he pulls away.

"They're napping," I tell him, my voice soft.."

"I want to see them," he says. There's a tenderness in him when he talks about the girls that gets me every time.

We head upstairs together, and the girls stir in their beds. Nico leans down beside them, his voice soft and full of warmth.

Lucia tugs on his arm. "Papa, will you bring us Christmas presents when you come back?"

He chuckles, shaking his head. "Christmas isn't for a few more days, sweetheart."

Giulia pipes up, grinning. "But we want presents now!"

Nico smiles, brushing a strand of hair from her face. "Tell you what—if you're good while I'm gone, maybe Santa will drop off an early present or two. But only if you're on your best behavior."

Their eyes light up, excitement bubbling over.. "Really?"

"Really," he says, leaning in. "But you have to listen to Willow and Ms. M, okay? No sneaking around trying to peek at presents early."

They nod eagerly, giggling at the idea of sneaking presents.

I watch from the doorway, my heart swelling with every word he says, every promise he makes. The way he talks to them, the love in his voice—it hits me hard every time.

The more I see him like this, the deeper I fall.

Nico says his goodbyes to the girls, giving them one last hug each, then as we're heading out of the room, he surprises me by pulling me in for a quick kiss.

The girls, of course, burst into giggles, making faces like it's the grossest thing ever. "Ewww, Papa, no kissing!"

I laugh along, but inside, my mind's doing flips. Does this mean Nico's ready to make whatever this is official? If so, I really need to drop the pregnancy bomb on him sooner rather than later.

Before he heads out, he turns back to the girls. "Be good for Willow, alright? I'll be back soon."

"Okay, Papa!" they chorus, waving at him with big smiles.

Nico gives me one last look that says a whole lot more than he's saying out loud before he leaves. My heart's still racing as I turn back to the girls.

"Alright, you two, I've got a surprise for you."

They sit up, instantly curious. "What is it?" Lucia asks, eyes wide.

"I was thinking after your nap, we could go to the park. And guess who's coming with us? My best friend in the whole world—my cousin Kendall."

Their faces light up, practically bouncing in their beds as they let out enthusiastic *yays*.

"Good, but first, nap time," I say, flicking off the light. They shut their eyes, clearly determined to get to the park as soon as possible.

I close the door quietly, but my thoughts are already somewhere else.

We're at the park with Kendall, and the girls are on a mission.

Their eyes are glued to the pond, scanning for ducks like their lives depend on it. Meanwhile, Kendall's next to me, raising an eyebrow. "You know all the ducks fly south for winter, right? They're probably halfway to Florida by now."

Lucia turns around, hands on her hips, all serious. "Some ducks stay. Our teacher says so."

"Yeah!" Giulia chimes in, nodding like she's backing up a science fact.

Kendall shrugs, clearly amused. "Alright, guess I've been schooled."

The girls proudly hold up their little baggies of rice, ready to feed the ducks. Kendall looks at them, then at me. "Wait, isn't rice bad for ducks? Doesn't it, like, make them, uh, explode or something?"

Lucia shakes her head, like she's heard this a million times. "Nope! That's not true. Ms. Julia at preschool said so."

I shrug, laughing a little. "Honestly, I thought the same thing, but apparently, it's an urban legend. Ducks are totally fine with rice. It's the bread you have to watch out for."

Kendall rubs the back of her neck, still not convinced. "Huh. Learn something new every day."

Just then, the girls start squealing. "Look! Ducks!" Sure enough, a couple of ducks waddle out from the pond, and the girls rush off with their bags of rice, beyond excited.

I watch them go, shaking my head.

"Told ya some ducks stay," Lucia says over her shoulder as the girls hurry off.

Kendall chuckles. "Yeah, yeah. Guess I need to learn preschool science."

The girls call out after Kendall, giggling as they trudge through the snow. "Kendall, you wanna help us feed the ducks?"

Kendall waves them off with a grin. "I'll help in a bit. I've got some stuff to talk about with Will."

The girls, totally unbothered, plod to the edge of the pond, happily tossing their rice to the ducks like it's the best day ever. Once they're out of earshot, Kendall turns to me, her eyes wide, practically buzzing with curiosity.

"Alright, spill the tea," she says, leaning in. "What's going on with Nico? Does he know about the *b-a-b-y*?"

I let out a long sigh. "No, he doesn't know. And honestly? I don't even know how to bring it up."

Kendall raises an eyebrow. "Girl, you're gonna have to tell him sooner or later. You can't just keep that kind of secret."

I rub my temples, feeling the stress building. "I know, I know. I almost told him today, but... I don't know. He's got a lot going on right now, and I don't want to make things worse."

Kendall gives me a look that says *I love you but get it together*. "Look, I get he's busy, but this isn't something you can just put off forever. You've got to tell him before it's too late."

I nod, knowing she's right, but I still feel like I'm in way over my head.

I glance at Kendall, biting my lip. "He's away on business or something right now. And it seemed serious."

Kendall's eyebrow shoots up. "*Business* as in Mob stuff?"

I tense, the memory of that day in the basement flashing back. "Yeah. I walked in on something I never should've seen. It scared the hell out of me."

Kendall leans in, her eyes widening. "What did you see?"

I take a deep breath. "Nico was... torturing someone. Right there in the basement. And the crazy thing is, even though it freaked me out, I still wanted him. Like, more than ever. The sex that night was on another level."

Kendall regards me with big, wide eyes. "Girl, are you telling me this whole lifestyle is turning you on?"

I shrug, feeling ridiculous but being completely honest. "I guess? I mean, I don't get it either. It's like, yeah, I should be running for the hills, but instead I'm falling harder."

Kendall shakes her head. "Look, I'm not here to judge. But I *am* here to tell you I want you, your baby, and those adorable little girls to be safe. Whatever happens with Nico, you need to make sure you're okay."

I nod, grateful for her looking out for me. "Thanks, Ken. I'm gonna tell him about the baby when he gets back. It's time."

Kendall squeezes my hand. "Good. He needs to know. Look, girl, follow your heart. It might take you to some wild places, like, you know, having a Mafia don's baby," she says with a wink, "but you've gotta listen to it, no matter how crazy it gets."

I chuckle, feeling a little lighter. Somehow, her words calm me down, like maybe I'm not completely losing my mind. "You're right. As usual."

Before we can talk any further, I hear a man's voice call out. "Willow?"

I turn, my heart skipping a beat. A sharply dressed man is standing a few dozen feet away, and the look on his face tells me something is very wrong. Instantly, my guard is up. He's closing the distance fast, worry written all over his features. My stomach twists.

"I'm sorry," he says, slightly out of breath when he reaches us. "Didn't mean to startle you, but... it's serious. Mr. Conti's been in an accident."

My blood runs cold, and the world seems to stop for a second. "What?"

He glances around, clearly nervous. "I can't explain here. You need to come with me."

I freeze, panic gripping my chest. Kendall steps closer, her face just as tense as mine. "What kind of accident?"

The man looks down, avoiding eye contact, and my heart feels like it's about to shatter. Everything in me is screaming that something's terribly wrong.

The guy brings his eyes back up to me. "I'll explain everything in the car."

I cross my arms, not budging. "Who are you? How do you know about Nico and who I am?"

He straightens, clearly not thrilled about having to give me answers. "Name's Enzo. I'm one of Sal's guys. He sent me to find you."

Sal. I know him. That name puts me a little at ease, but not much. I glance at Kendall, then back at Enzo. "I'll get the girls, and we'll go."

Enzo shakes his head. "It'd be better if your friend took the girls home. This isn't a place for them."

Tension shoots through me, my mind racing. Kendall steps up beside me, her hand on my arm. "We're only ten minutes away, and Olivia said she'd be home by the time we got back, right?"

I hesitate but nod. "Yeah."

Kendall gives me a reassuring look. "We'll be fine. Go handle this."

I swallow hard and call out to the girls. They run over, bright-eyed and curious. I kneel, trying to keep my voice steady. "Kendall's going to take you home, okay? I have to go with Mr. Enzo."

They both look worried, but Giulia grabs Lucia's hand. "Okay."

They turn to go with Kendall, and I feel a pang of guilt.

I watch as Kendall and the girls cross Central Park West, keeping my eyes on them until they disappear from view. Kendall's got them, I remind myself, trying to calm the storm brewing inside me. But my nerves are on edge, and Enzo's in a hurry, practically pulling me through the park.

"What kind of accident?" I press, my voice shaky.

"We need to get to the car," he says, not slowing down.." He doesn't slow down as he speaks. "I'll explain everything on the way to the hospital."

Hospital. The word alone sends my mind spinning. My heart's pounding, and all I can think is, *Did Nico's lifestyle finally catch up to him? Is this what happens when you fall for someone like him?*

We reach his car, a sleek black SUV parked at the curb. Enzo opens the passenger door, gesturing for me to get in. I hesitate for a split second, but he's alone, which gives me a small sense of comfort.

I slide in, and my thoughts are so consumed by worry for Nico that I barely register anything else. Enzo climbs into the driver's seat, and the second he starts the engine, I hear the click of the doors locking.

The anxiety is clawing at me from the inside, and I feel like I'm barely holding it together.

CHAPTER 29

NICO

I'm sitting in my office at the warehouse in Yonkers, tapping my fingers on the desk. The space is bare—just a desk, some shelves, and an overstuffed couch that's seen better days but works fine for crashing. It's simple, functional, nothing fancy, but it serves its purpose.

Still, I can't shake this itch under my skin. I'm ready for action. I know I need to be prudent, make calculated moves, but sitting on the brink of conflict and not being able to strike yet is nearly impossible to tolerate. My instincts are screaming to make the next move, but the timing has to be right.

I lean back, thinking about the Rossis. If they orchestrated my father's assassination, they knew it would trigger war, which means they're ready for it, maybe even more prepared than we are. But I'll be damned if I let that stop me. This conflict is inevitable, and I'll make sure we come out on top. Failure isn't an option.

My jaw tightens as I think it over. The more I dwell on it, the more I realize how deep this is going to go. The Rossis knew exactly what they were setting into motion, and that means they've planned for every move I could make.

But I'll outmaneuver them. I have to.

A knock at the door snaps me out of my thoughts. I grab the Glock off my desk, approaching the door with the kind of caution that's second nature by now. Before I can ask who it is, a voice calls through the door.

"It's Sal. I'm not alone—I've got a little present for you."

I keep the gun in hand as I unlock the door and swing it open. Sal's standing there, but it's the sight behind him that grabs my attention. Two of his guys are holding up a beat-up schmuck, blood all over his face, his arms pinned by the goons on either side of him.

I narrow my eyes. "What the hell is this?"

Sal grins like he's just handed me a gift wrapped in red and gold. "This, my friend, is the man who planned the hit on your father. The one who pulled the trigger."

I say nothing for a moment as I size the guy up. He's not Jack—that much is clear. My grip tightens on the Glock as I take in the sight of him, this pathetic excuse for a man who thinks he's walking out of here alive.

"Let's take him to the conference room," I say coldly.."

We move as a group to the conference room next to the office. My men shove the guy into a chair, binding him tight. I step back, my mind already working through what's coming next.

The guy's face is swollen and bloodied, but that means nothing to me. I glance at Sal again. "You sure this is the guy? The one who shot my father?"

Sal nods, confidence in his voice. "Yeah, this is him."

I snort, shaking my head. "Well, that was fucking easy."

I turn my attention back to the man. He's got fear in his eyes, and the gag in his mouth is soaked with blood. He knows what's coming. I raise the Glock so he can see it, turning it over in my hand, watching his face pale even more.

"Listen," I start, my voice cold and measured. "I'm a busy man. I've got a lot going on, and I don't have time for bullshit." I take a step closer, the gun still in view. "You're going to talk and let me be real clear—if you bullshit me, waste my time, or even *think* about playing games, I'll put a bullet in your skull without a second thought."

I let that sink in for a moment. "Now, I'm going to take off the gag, but I want you to think *very* carefully about each little word that comes out of your mouth. Because any one of them could be your last. Understand?"

The guy nods frantically, eyes wide with panic.

"Good," I say, satisfied, ripping the gag off and tossing it to the side. "Start talking."

"It wasn't me!" The words burst out of the guy's mouth in a desperate plea.

I can't help but laugh, and the rest of the guys follow. The sound echoes off the walls like a death sentence. Without a second thought, I backhand him hard across the face. His head snaps to the side.

"I should've known you'd start with that bullshit."," I say, my voice low and cold.

The guy's shaking, clearly terrified, but he keeps talking. "I was set up by the Rossis. They needed a scapegoat for the hit, and I—"

I turn to Sal, raising an eyebrow. "Where the hell did you find this prick?"

Sal steps forward, arms crossed. "One of my contacts in the Rossi network heard about a payout. Tracked this guy down in the middle of getting a fat payday. Picked him up right after." He smirks. "We've got the money too, boss, if you want it."

I nod slowly, thenI turn my attention back to the guy in the chair. His lip is split, his eyes wild with fear, but I'm not buying any of it. He's just a piece on the board, and right now, I'm deciding whether to keep him around or toss him aside.

I lean in. , my eyes locked on the man, every muscle in my body ready to move. "Let's talk about the money," I say. "You got paid for a hit but didn't actually pull the trigger?"

He shakes his head so fast it's pathetic. "No, no, that's not it. I was getting paid for some gun running I did earlier that month. Just business."

I watch him closely. , picking apart every word, every twitch in his face. "So, what you're saying is the payment was meant to *look* like it was for the hit. And someone sent bad info down the channels to pin it on you?"

He nods again, swallowing hard. "Yeah. That's exactly what happened."

I narrow my eyes. "Why? Why go through all that trouble?"

He hesitates, like he's searching for a way out, but there's none. Not here. Finally, he says, "The Rossis know war's coming. They must think if you find the guy behind the hit, maybe you'll call it off—or at least delay it. They're playing you."

I pause, considering his words carefully. If the Rossis are scrambling to throw me off, it means they're not as eager for war as I thought. Maybe they're stalling, trying to buy time. Either way, this changes things – if it's true.

The room is silent except for the sound of the man's ragged breathing. I nod to Sal, signaling him to step outside with me. "Stay with him," I tell his men, glancing at the guy, who's still sweating and looking like he's two seconds away from breaking.

Sal follows me into the hallway, shutting the door behind us. I turn to him, keeping my voice low but firm. "How certain are you that your info's solid?"

Sal sighs, rubbing the back of his neck. "It came from a reliable contact; someone I've worked with for years. But," he adds, "if that contact was fed bad intel, it complicates things."

I rake a hand through my hair, the tension building. "I don't like being deceived, Sal. If someone's trying to play me, that's a bigger problem than we thought."

Sal nods. "I get it. But here's the thing—the guy knows he's two minutes away from a bullet in his skull and his body floating in the East River. He could be spinning whatever bullshit he thinks will keep him alive." He grins, a little too eager. "We could always torture it out of him. Might speed things up."

I shake my head, crossing my arms. "Not yet. I don't want to go that far unless we have to. Let's keep our options open."

Sal shrugs, clearly disappointed, but he knows I'm right. There's a balance between getting answers and creating chaos, and right now, I need clarity—not more blood.

I nod toward the door, and Sal catches the signal, following me back into the room. The man looks like a cornered animal. The fear in his eyes tells me everything—he thinks we've made the call to put him down.

I step slowly toward him, not breaking eye contact as I approach. The tension in the room thickens, and his breathing gets shallow. I stand over him, taking my time before I speak.

"What's your relationship to the Rossis? Exactly."

He swallows hard, stammering. "I'm just a low-level guy. I swear, nothing big." He glances between me and Sal, then quickly adds, "But not anymore. I'm done working for people that'd throw one of their own to the wolves like this."

I tilt my head, studying him. His desperation is clear, but I'm not buying it yet.

He keeps going, trying to talk his way out. "If I make it out of here alive, I'm done with the Rossis. I'll ditch 'em, leave town, whatever it takes."

I crouch down in front of him, close enough that he can feel the weight of my presence. "That's a big 'if,'" I say quietly, my voice carrying more threat than any shout ever could.

He's shaking now, eyes wide. I keep my gaze locked on him. "Here's the deal—you're going to give me information. Good information. On the Rossis." I lean in just a little closer. "Your life depends on it."

CHAPTER 30

I'm sitting in the back of the car, watching the city blur past, trying to make sense of everything. It doesn't take long for me to realize something's off. We're not headed toward any hospital I know of.

My stomach tightens with unease. I lean forward, clearing my throat. "Enzo, where are we going?"

He doesn't respond, just keeps his eyes on the road, jaw clenched.

I try again, this time with more edge in my voice. "Hey, I asked you a question—where the hell are we going?"

"Keep quiet," he snaps, not even looking at me.

That's when it hits me. I'm in trouble.

I reach for my phone, heart pounding now. I need to call someone—*anyone*—but the second I pull it out, Enzo turns in his seat, snatching it from my hand before I even have a chance to unlock it. My mouth drops open in shock, but it gets worse—he rolls down the window and tosses it out without a second thought.

"What the fuck?" I shout, rattled.

He doesn't even look at me, just rolls the window back up like nothing happened. I sit back, my mind racing. I'm trapped, and whatever I thought was happening is clearly much worse than I imagined.

I let out a full-on, horror-movie scream that fills the entire car. It's loud, shrill, and completely over-the-top, but it's the only thing I can do right now. Enzo winces, groaning in pain, one hand flying to his ear while he keeps the other on the wheel.

I'm terrified, but I keep screaming, partly because I'm scared out of my mind and partly because it's the only way I can fight back at this moment.

"Cut it out!" he snaps, trying to shout over me.

I ignore him and suck in another breath, my voice going louder. "Let me go!" I scream, yanking on the door handle, but of course, it's locked and won't budge while the car's moving. My heart's racing, my hands shaking, but I don't stop. I keep yelling and pulling at the door, trying to make as much noise as humanly possible.

Enzo's losing it. ", his knuckles white on the steering wheel. "Shut up!" he yells, his voice sharp and pissed off, but I don't care. I keep going, louder and more frantic, hoping to throw him off his game, mess with his head. He's clearly getting angrier by the second, his jaw clenched tight. The more pissed off he gets, the louder I scream. It's the only thing I can do, and I'm not stopping.

Finally, Enzo snaps. He reaches over and smacks me across the face, and the sting of it is immediate, shutting me up on the spot. I'm stunned—I've never been hit like that before—and for a second, all I can do is sit there, frozen. But as the shock fades, pure anger takes over. *Hell no.* My mind clears, and before I can even think about it, I ball my hand into a fist and punch him as hard as I can in the jaw.

He yells in pain, the car swerving wildly across lanes. My heart's thumping as I watch him struggle to get the car back under control, and for a split second, I feel a rush of triumph.

But it doesn't last long.

Once the car is steady, he turns to me with fury in his eyes and reaches over, grabbing me by the hair. I let out a gasp as he yanks my head back, his grip tight and painful.

"If you don't sit still and shut up," he snarls, voice low and dangerous, "I'll *make* you be quiet."

The threat in his voice is clear, and my heart skips a beat. He's not playing around, and I know now just how serious this is. I stay silent, my mind racing, but the fire in my chest is still burning. If he thinks I'm just going to sit here and do nothing, he's dead wrong.

I want to hit the bastard again, feel that surge of adrenaline rush through me. But then I remember—*the baby.* I have to keep it together, no matter how much I want to fight back. Stressing myself out or risking another blow isn't worth it. I take a few deep breaths, trying to calm the rage bubbling inside me.

Enzo smirks, glancing at me from the corner of his eye. "Ah, finally figured out it's better to shut the fuck up, huh? Smart girl."

I bite my tongue, holding back the flood of insults sitting on the tip of it. It's not worth setting him off again.

He keeps going, clearly enjoying his little power trip. "That was your one warning. Pull another stunt like that, and I'll tie you up and throw you in the trunk. Maybe you'll run out of air, maybe you won't. Wanna take that chance?"

My blood runs cold, but my face is steady as I rub the spot on my head where he pulled at my hair. "Where are you taking me?"

He doesn't even hesitate. "Some important people want to have a chat with you. Seems they're real interested in your relationship with Nico Conti."

The pit in my stomach tightens.

I wrap my arms around my middle, like it'll somehow protect me from whatever this asshole throws my way next. It's not just about staying calm anymore—it's about survival, for me and my baby. "I don't know anything about Nico," I say, trying to sound firm. "I'm just the nanny for his girls. That's it."

Enzo lets out a low, mocking laugh.

"What's so funny?" I snap, even though my pulse is pounding in my ears.?"

He smirks, glancing at me like he's got some dirty little secret. "I've seen you doing a hell of a lot more than nanny duties, sweetheart."

It takes a second for his words to click, but when they do, it feels like a punch to the gut. He's *seen* us. My face burns with a mix of anger and disgust.

"You're a sick fuck," I spit, my voice low and venomous.."

Enzo just laughs, that twisted smile never leaving his face. "Call me whatever you want. Just keep your mouth shut if you want to get out of this alive."

The horror of it all sinks in—someone's been watching us. The realization makes me go quiet, my mind racing.

I need to think. I need to figure out how to get myself out of this. Because if they know about Nico and me, then this is much bigger than I thought.

CHAPTER 31

"Your life depends on giving me something useful. I suggest you choose your next words carefully."

I lean in closer, my voice cold and steady.

The man's sweating like a pig, his eyes darting around the room, looking for an escape that isn't there. He's trembling, and it's clear he's close to breaking. But I can tell he's holding back. He knows something, and he's trying to decide if it's worth spilling.

"You're holding out on me," I say, my gaze locked on him. "I can see it. Don't think you're smart enough to play this game with me."

Sal, reading the situation perfectly, pulls his gun and presses it against the man's head. "Time's up. You tell us what we need to know, or you die right here. No one's coming to save you."

His eyes widen, darting between Sal and me. He's shaking like a leaf, knowing he's got no good options left. He turns to me, his voice cracking. "You won't find out anything if I die."

I narrow my eyes, watching him closely. He's bluffing—or trying to—but the fear in his voice tells me otherwise. He's got something, something important. He just needs a little more pressure to crack.

He's close, and I know he's about to spill. I start counting down, my voice cold and steady. "Three..."

He's panicking, stammering out useless excuses. "I-I don't know! I swear!"

"Two..."

He's sweating bullets now, his voice shaking. "Please, I'll tell you everything!"

"One..."

Just as I'm about to hit zero, the guy breaks. "*Jack!*"

I pause my grip on the situation tightening. "Jack?"

"Yeah, Jack," he says, nodding frantically, like he's finally decided to save his own skin. "Jack Swinson."

The name hits me like a sledgehammer, my blood starting to boil. My face is blank, but inside, I'm ready to snap.

"Describe him," I say, keeping my voice even.

He swallows hard. "Young guy, good looking, long, stringy hair... he's—he's the one. He's been working with the Rossis."

I had him in my fucking basement, within reach, and now my blood's burning hotter than ever.

I take a step back, letting the anger simmer just below the surface. The guy's lucky he's still breathing, but now I've got the name I need.

Sal's face twists in rage, knowing Jack slipped through our fingers because of him. He looks like he's ready to tear the poor schmuck apart. He steps toward him, fists clenched, but I stop him, throwing out an arm.

"Not yet," I tell him. "I haven't decided if I'm gonna kill him, but he's bought himself a little more time."

Sal's nostrils flare, and he shoots a venomous look at the guy. "You're not off the hook," he growls, his voice low and dangerous. "Not even close."

I grab Sal by the arm and guide him out into the hallway. The men stay inside, guarding our guest while I shut the door behind us.

"Listen," I say, my voice sharp. "Contact everyone. Put a price on Jack Swinson's head— alive. We need him breathing when he's brought to me."

Sal nods, already reaching for his phone. "How much are we talking?"

"Enough to make him impossible to hide. We end this."

Sal pulls out his phone, but curses under his breath. "No bars."

"Yeah, reception's generally shitty in this place."

"I'll take care of it outside," he says, turning on his heel and heading for the door.

I watch him go, the tension in my chest tightening. Alone in the hallway, I let the silence settle for a moment, my mind already racing with the next move.

Jack's still out there—and when I find him, I'll end him. Letting him out of my sight won't be a mistake I make twice.

Once I'm alone, the rage takes over. I slam my fist into the wall, the crack echoing through the hallway. The plaster splits, pain shooting up my hand, but I don't care.

I take a slow, deep breath, trying to calm myself. *Focus.* Losing control now won't help anything.

What if they don't find him?

I shake the thought off. There's no use worrying about things that haven't happened yet. We're going to find him. And when we do, he'll wish I'd killed him the first time he was in my basement.

With my anger under control, I head back into the room. I stand over the Rossi stooge, my expression cold and hard.

"Here's the deal," I begin. "Whether or not you live or die depends on one thing—whether the information you gave me about Jack turns out to be true."

His eyes widen even more, and I can see him calculating his chances. He knows his life is hanging by a thread, and I'm the one holding the scissors.

I lean in closer, my voice cold and deliberate. ""Here's how it's gonna go, prick. If your information checks out, you'll make it out of this alive. Hell, I'll even pay for your flight out of town so you can run from the Rossis. But if you're bullshitting me..." I trail off, letting the threat hang heavy in the air.

His eyes dart around, frantic. "I'm not! I swear I'm not lying! It's the truth!"

"We'll find out. ," I say, my tone sharp. "One way or another."

I glance at the guards in the room and nod toward them. "Until then, you're staying right here with your new friends. They'll either be your executioners or your oh-so-charming escorts out of the city. The choice is yours."

His face pales even more, sweat dripping down his forehead. I can see him panicking, trying to figure out if there's any way to talk himself out of this.

"If you've got anything else to tell me about Jack," I say, "now's the time."

He swallows hard, panic all over his face, then blurts out, "Jack's got a place in the Bronx. Hunts Point, near Spofford and Manida Street. Three-story building with blue trim. That's where the Rossis meet him."

"Rough part of town." I narrow my eyes. "They meet him there?"

The man nods quickly, desperate. "Yeah, yeah. I've heard them talk about it."

I stand up straight, letting the silence stretch for a moment before turning to leave. *This better be true.*

I step out of the room, tossing a quick command over my shoulder to the men. "Wait for my call. Don't do anything until I give the word."

As I make my way down the hallway, something tugs at the back of my mind. I haven't checked my phone in hours. It's been sitting dead in my pocket, no reception in this godforsaken warehouse. I pull it out and glance at the screen—still no bars. I curse under my breath and push open the door, stepping outside. The cold air hits me immediately, biting at my skin, but I barely notice.

Off in the distance, I see Sal on his phone, pacing back and forth. The sky above is thick with gray clouds, heavy and ready to dump more snow. There's a tension in the air, something ominous. It's not just the weather, either.

As I move away from the building, reception starts to creep back. My phone lights up with missed calls, a flood of notifications filling the screen. Ms. M. Texts, voicemails—dozens of them.

A strange feeling washes over me. *Something's wrong.* My instincts scream it loud and clear. All I can think about is home—the girls, Willow. Those domestic feelings, ones I haven't felt in years, rush back hard and fast. I should be with them.

I don't bother sifting through the texts or voicemails. My gut's already twisted tight. I hit call on Ms. M's number, and she picks up on the first ring.

"Nico," she says, her voice tense. "It's Willow. She's missing."

I hear a younger voice in the background, and then someone takes the phone. "Nico? This is Kendall, Willow's cousin," she says quickly, her words rushing out. "I was with her at the park."

232 | K.C. CROWNE

"What happened?" My voice is low, dangerous. Every muscle in my body tenses as I wait for her explanation.

"We were with the girls, feeding ducks in the park. Some guy came up to us—said something happened to you. He told Willow it was an emergency, and she went with him. She sent the girls home with me."

My blood boils. Every word she says cranks the rage tighter and tighter inside me, burning like fire. "The girls?" I ask, barely controlling the fury in my voice.

"They're safe. He didn't touch them," Kendall says, her voice shaking.

I clench my jaw, the rage seething inside. Some piece of shit has Willow, and he'll pay for it with his life.

"Do you know who this guy was?" I growl, already forming a list of who's going to die.

"He said his name was Enzo, but that could be a lie."

I don't say another word. I hang up, my mind already going dark with thoughts of vengeance.

I spot Sal wrapping up his call, and I stride over, my fury barely contained. "Willow's missing," I say, my voice sharp as a knife.

Sal's eyes widen, rage flickering across his face. "Fuck, Nico. I—damn it. This is on me. I screwed up letting Jack get away."

I shake my head, shutting that down. "We don't have time for that now. What matters is figuring out who the fuck took Willow. And I'm damn sure Jack's involved. It all fits."

Sal grits his teeth, fists clenched. "What's the play?"

"We're going to the Bronx," I say, the words cold and final. "Get four of our heaviest hitters—no more fuckups. This ends now."

Sal nods, already pulling out his phone again. "I'll have the guys ready in ten."

I don't bother waiting for a response, already moving. My mind is set, focused. Jack Swinson made this personal, and now I'm going to end him.

This is bigger than business. Bigger than revenge. Willow's involved now, and whoever thought they could touch what's mine is about to learn a painful lesson.

Sal finishes his call and nods at me. "They'll meet us in the Bronx. We're bringing everything we've got."

"Good. We'll finish this once and for all."

CHAPTER 32

I'm in a total daze as we drive. My mind's racing, but all I can think about is the girls.

God, I hope they made it home safe.

And the baby—I can't help but worry about what this stress is doing to the tiny life inside me. My hands instinctively go to my stomach, trying to calm the fear bubbling up.

We're heading into Queens now, the streets unfamiliar, and nothing about this feels right. I glance at the driver, asking a question as if he'll answer me. "Where are you taking me?"

"Shut the fuck up," he snaps, not even bothering to look at me.

My stomach tightens with dread. We finally pull up to a rundown townhouse in a sketchy part of the Bronx. The neighborhood's rough, graffiti on every wall, the place looking like it's barely standing.

Enzo parks, gets out, and comes around to open the door. But I don't wait for him to grab me. The second that door opens, I lunge forward and slam my forehead into his face, hard.

"*Fuck!*" he yells, stumbling back, clutching his nose.

I bolt out of the car, running as fast as I can. My feet hit the pavement, and I don't even know where I'm going, but it doesn't matter. I just need to get away. Luckily, there isn't as much snow as there was at Nico's.

I'm running as hard as I can, but it's tough with my wrists bound. My breath's ragged, heart pounding like it's about to burst out of my chest. I keep pushing, legs burning, turning the corner with a sliver of hope that I might actually get away.

But it's a ghost town. Desolate. Nothing but abandoned buildings, and not a single person in sight. The panic sets in deeper.

Behind me, I hear the guy from the car yelling for help. I glance over my shoulder and see two huge dudes barreling after me, running way faster than I thought possible for guys their size.

Shit.

I push harder, my lungs screaming, but just when I think I might have a shot at outrunning them, my foot slips. I hit a patch of ice and go down hard on my side, the impact slamming into my shoulder like a sledgehammer. The pain is instant, radiating through my entire arm. I gasp, trying to suck in air, but it feels like everything's spinning.

Flat on my back, all I can see is the slate gray sky above, cold and unforgiving. The pounding of footsteps is getting louder, closer, and there's nothing I can do.

I scramble to my feet, trying to shake off the pain and get another run in, but it's too late. The guys are on me in seconds. One of them pulls out a knife, holding it inches from my face.

"You need to fucking behave," he growls.

The other one grabs me by the arm, yanking me upright like I weigh nothing. My heart's still racing, fear and adrenaline surging through me. They drag me back toward the corner, where the driver is waiting, a nasty smirk on his face. Without warning, he backhands me hard, the sting spreading across my cheek.

"Don't try that shit again."

Dazed, I barely process what's happening as they march me toward the rundown house. The driver calls out, "Cobra," like it's some secret code or password.

The door swings open, and on the other side is an absolute mountain of a man, easily twice my size. He looks me over, grunting, then nods for the others to bring me inside.

To my surprise, the inside isn't some abandoned crack house like I expected. It's buzzing with activity. Guys huddled over tables, weighing out bags of drugs, others stacking crates full of guns. The place is crawling with criminals, all moving with purpose.

I'm led deeper into the house, and I can feel the eyes of some of these criminals crawling over me like I'm meat on display. My skin crawls. Part of me wants to snap, to tell them to keep their disgusting stares to themselves, but I keep my mouth shut. I can't risk getting roughed up, not with the baby to think about. I'm already freaked about the fall I took a few minutes ago.

We walk through a narrow hallway and into an office. I'm still trying to make sense of everything when I freeze. Sitting there, battered and bruised, is the man I saw in Nico's basement. His face is a mess—bruises covering every inch—and when he grins at me, I notice he's missing a tooth.

Nico didn't kill him. The thought hits me, and for a second, there's a weird sense of relief. At least until the man opens his mouth.

"Well, well, well... look what we have here." His voice is slimy, full of dark amusement. "You'll do nicely for bait."

My stomach drops. *Bait?* They're using me to get to Nico.

I try to keep my expression neutral, but inside, panic's clawing at me. This guy isn't just some low-level thug. He's the reason Nico's been so on edge.

And now I'm right in the middle of it.

He rises from behind the desk, his eyes locking onto mine, a disgusting sneer spreading across his bruised face. Every step he takes closer, the more I can see just how wrecked his face is.

Nico really did a number on him. If only he were here to finish the job.

"You're all mine now," he says, his voice dripping with twisted satisfaction.."

I try to raise my hand, instinctively wanting to slap that smug grin off his face. But my wrists are still bound.

He sees me struggle and laughs, the sound low and menacing. His breath reeks as he leans in closer, his face inches from mine. The way he looks at me, like he's already won, makes my skin crawl. I can feel it in his eyes—he's completely unhinged.

"Not so tough now, huh?"

One of his goons steps forward at his nod and grabs my bindings. He jerks me back so hard I nearly stumble, the force sending a sharp pain through my shoulders. I gasp, my teeth gritted, trying to hold back any sound of pain. I won't give him the satisfaction.

But inside I'm scared as hell. This guy's nuts, and I have no idea what he's planning. All I know is that whatever it is, it's bad. I can only hope Nico's on his way.

I spit right in his face, nailing him on the cheek. For a split second, a wild rage flashes in his eyes, and I swear I've just sealed my fate. I barely have time to process it before he pulls out a gun, waving it in front of my face. My heart slams against my chest, but I hold my ground, trying not to let him see the fear crawling up my spine.

"You just used your one fuck-up," he snarls, his voice dripping with venom. He wipes the spit off his cheek with a wicked grin. "The name's Jack. And for now, you're my property."

Property? The word makes my skin crawl, but I keep my mouth shut this time. No need to push my luck again.

Jack steps closer, his eyes dark and dangerous. "What do you think of my face, huh?" He points to his bruises, the busted-up mess Nico left him with.

I stare him down, my voice steady despite the fear thrumming through me. "I think you must've deserved it for Nico to do that to you."

Jack throws his head back and laughs, a twisted, humorless sound. "Oh, sweetheart, when I'm done with you, I'm gonna look like a fucking model in comparison."

The threat hangs in the air, heavy and real. I try to stay strong, but I can feel the walls closing in. I switch gears, going for the clueless, innocent vibe. "Why me?" I ask, trying to sound like I'm not as scared as I am.

Jack grins, and it's creepy as hell. "Hurting a man physically? That's basic," he says, stepping closer, his gross gaze locked on me. "But getting to his woman? Hurting her? That wrecks him. Makes him lose control. Nico will be so blinded by rage that he won't be thinking straight. Easy pickings."

"You've got it twisted. I'm just the nanny. Mr. Conti doesn't care what happens to me. At most, he's got to deal with the hassle of hiring a new one."

Jack stares at me, his grin fading into something darker. I hold my breath, praying he buys my act. If Nico doesn't show up soon, I'm not sure how much longer I can keep up this front.

He leans in, way too close, making my skin crawl. I squirm, trying to pull back, but there's nowhere to go. His breath is hot and disgusting as it fans across my face.

"You're not *just* the nanny, sweetheart. I know everything," he says, his voice low and slimy. "I've seen what you and Nico get down to when the girls are asleep."

My blood runs cold, a wave of panic washing over me.

He knows.

He's seen us.

Jack gets even closer, his lips near my ear, and I can feel his breath on my skin. "Gotta say," he whispers, "I loved watching your little exercise routine in Conti's home gym."

A wave of disgust hits me, and I have to fight the urge to throw up. Embarrassment, fear, and fury mix into this painful, swirling mess inside me, but my expression is cold when I look at him. I'm not giving this creep the satisfaction of seeing me break. I glare at him, my jaw clenched tight. He's waiting for me to freak out, to cry, but I'm not going to give him what he wants. He can play his sick little games, but I'm stronger than that.

Jack looks at me like I'm some kind of toy he's deciding whether to break. His gaze lingers on the dried blood from my busted lip, his lips twisting into an amused smirk.

"Hmm," he muses, tilting his head like he's deep in thought. "Do you look rough enough to really scare Conti? I don't know."

My vision goes hazy for a second, my body going cold. *He's serious.* The thought alone makes me feel faint, but I grit my teeth and force myself to stay conscious. I will not pass out in front of him.

He lets his sadistic little statement hang in the air, enjoying the fear he knows I'm trying to hide. Then, after what feels like forever, he laughs. "Maybe if I get bored."

Without warning, he grabs my chin roughly, forcing my face toward his. The sudden pressure makes my heart race, but I hold his gaze, determined not to show weakness.

He pulls out his phone, smirks, and prepares to snap a pic.

"*Smile.*"

CHAPTER 33

NICO

"Faster."

I sit in the passenger seat, my jaw clenched tight, fists balled in my lap. Normally, I'd be the one driving, but I'm so fucking pissed off I know I'd end up driving us straight into a wall.

Sal's at the wheel, keeping his eyes on the road as the sky darkens around us, the mood getting heavier by the minute. Behind us is another car with four of my best guys—my heaviest hitters. I'm ready for whatever comes next. This isn't just about taking Jack out anymore. It's about getting Willow back. *My woman.*

I know it now, with absolute certainty—I love her.

The thought of losing her, of not getting the chance to tell her how I feel, twists in my gut. It's almost too much to bear, but I push it down. I have to stay focused. I have to get her back. *I will* get her back. Whatever it takes.

Just as I'm caught in that spiral of thoughts, my phone buzzes in my pocket. I pull my phone from my pocket, seeing an unknown *number* flash on the screen. Normally, I'd ignore it, but another message comes through, and then another. Something feels off, so I open them.

What I see makes my blood turn to fire. It's Willow, her eyes full of fear. She's pulled into a twisted selfie with Jack, that smug bastard grinning like he's already won.

My grip tightens on the phone, and for a second, I'm ready to crush it in my hand. The rage inside me is like nothing I've ever felt before. My heart pounds, my mind racing with violent thoughts.

Sal glances over at me, sensing the shift. "What is it?"

I show him the screen, and he lets out a low curse, his knuckles going white around the steering wheel. "That motherfucker."

He doesn't need to say it, but we both know now—Jack's behind it all. This isn't just business. It's personal.

Sal's voice cuts through the anger clouding my head. "Look, Nico. Jack's trying to mess with you. He's throwing you off your game, and you can't fall for it. He wants you to lose control."

I grit my teeth, barely able to keep the fury in check. But I know Sal's right. Jack's playing his little mind games, and if I let him get to me, it'll be exactly what he wants.

Sal glances at me, his brow furrowed in confusion. "Why would Jack go after the nanny like that?"

I don't respond, just grit my teeth, the rage simmering under the surface. Sal's no idiot, though. He looks at me, nodding slowly as it clicks.

"She's not just the nanny, is she?"

I let out a slow, measured breath, trying to keep myself steady. "If Jack so much as touches her..." I trail off, my voice low, dangerous. "He's going to take up permanent residence in my basement."

The thought of what I'll do to Jack when I get him is already flashing through my mind, but first, I need to make sure Willow's safe. That's all that matters right now.

"Speed up," I bark, and Sal doesn't hesitate, putting his foot down as we cross the Third Avenue Bridge into the Bronx. The festive Christmas lights around the city flash by, their cheery glow feeling like some twisted joke compared to what I'm going through. There's no peace in this holiday season. Not for me.

Sal glances over again, his hands tight on the wheel. "Maybe text back? See what Jack's planning."

I clench my jaw. He's right. As much as I hate playing into Jack's sick game, I need to know what he wants. I take out my phone, my fingers hovering over the screen.

I text back. *Where are you?*

The reply comes almost instantly, an address lighting up my screen. My eyes narrow as I recognize it—it matches the info the stooge gave us earlier. I plug the address into the car's GPS.

More texts come in, taunting messages meant to piss me off, to rattle me.

Bet you didn't think I'd have the balls to take her.

She's real cute when she's scared, you know.

Think she'll cry if I touch her? Or is she tougher than that?

C'mon, Nico. Say something. You're not gonna let me have all the fun, are you?

My hand tightens around the phone. Every word's designed to piss me off, to get under my skin. But I don't bite. Jack wants me to lose control, to make a mistake. I won't give him the satisfaction. Willow's life is on the line, and I need to stay focused.

You don't know what you've gotten yourself into, you dumb fuck, I think to myself, but I keep my fingers off the keys.

We drive deeper into the Bronx, the streets getting rougher. Graffiti-covered walls, busted-out windows, and abandoned lots. It's the kind of neighborhood where you don't ask questions, and no one offers answers. The buildings loom tall and worn down, barely holding themselves together.

I look out the window, my blood boiling but my mind sharp. We're close now. This is Jack's territory, but soon, it's going to be *my* battlefield.

Sal glances at me, sensing the shift. "You good?"

I nod, my voice low and cold. "I'm ready."

My patience is wearing thin, every text from Jack lighting me up inside. The urge to tear him apart is damn near unbearable, but I can't lose it—not yet. Then, a thought hits me.

"Pull over," I tell Sal.

He glances at me but doesn't hesitate, guiding the car to the side of the road. The car with our heavies behind us follows suit, pulling up just a few feet back.

Sal turns to me. "What's up?"

I stare out the window for a second, piecing together the plan in my head. "There's a damn good chance Jack kills Willow the second we burst through the door."

Sal's face tightens. He knows I'm right. "Yeah. So, what's the move?"

I pause, then meet his eyes. "We can't go in there guns blazing. Jack's expecting that, probably counting on it. We need a smarter play."

Sal nods slowly. "What are you thinking?"

I lean back in my seat, the anger swirling inside me but my mind locked in.

"I've got an idea."

CHAPTER 34

I'm still stuck in this dingy office with Jack, trying hard to hide my fear. It feels like I've been here for hours, but it's probably only been one. Still no sign of Nico. My heart's pounding, but my expression is calm.

Jack leans back in his chair, smirking like he's already won. "Maybe you were right," he says, his voice dripping with arrogance.. " Maybe he really doesn't care about you."

I glare at him, refusing to let him see me sweat. "You don't know anything about Nico," I snap, though my heart clenches with worry.

He'll come for me. But what if he gets hurt?

I turn to Jack, my voice sharper than I feel. "Why the hell are you doing this? What's your plan here, huh?"

Jack grins at me like he's been waiting for that question all night. "Ah, finally," he says, leaning back in his chair. "You wanna know why?"

I narrow my eyes, not liking the way he's enjoying this. "Yeah, why?"

"There's been a war brewing between the Rossis and the Contis for a long, long time," he starts, his grin widening. "Even before I took out Nico's old man. But frankly, it's been too quiet. Too peaceful. This city needs a good war. And so do I."

I raise an eyebrow, trying to hide my confusion. "Need a war? Why the hell would you *need* one?"

Jack chuckles, clearly loving the sound of his own voice. "Because, sweetheart, I'm a free agent. A guy who gets people things—whatever they need. And when there's peace between the families, business is slow. Not as profitable as it could be." He leans in closer, his eyes gleaming with greed. "Just like with wars between countries, there's tons of money to be made when the bullets start flying. Both sides need weapons, supplies, and they'll pay top dollar to make sure they have the upper hand."

I'm starting to piece it together, and it makes me sick. He's not just some thug—he's a war profiteer.

I can't believe what I'm hearing. "That's it?" I ask, my voice dripping with disbelief. "All this... just for money?"

Jack chuckles, leaning back in his chair like I'm some naive kid. "What else is there?" he shoots back. "Easy for you to judge. You're living on easy street, thanks to Nico's dime. And Nico? His position was handed to him by his old man. Men like me? We come from nothing. We have to claw our way up."

I shake my head, trying to make sense of his twisted logic. "So, what? That makes this okay? People are going to die because of you."

He shrugs, completely unbothered. "The game's been dirty long before I showed up. Drug running, trafficking, all kinds of slimy shit. Just because Nico's pops cleaned up their image and got them out of the seedier parts doesn't make them angels."

I glare at him, my fists clenching at my sides. "That doesn't mean it's right. You're still responsible for those deaths."

Jack laughs again, a cold, heartless sound. "People have *already* died, sweetheart. What's a few more dozen?"

The casual way he says it sends chills down my spine.

Jack leans in, a sick grin spreading across his face. "But there's more to this game than just money," he says, his voice dripping with menace. "I've been following you, sweetheart. Tailin' you, watching you and Nico have a little fun."

I glare at him, disgusted.

He laughs, clearly enjoying this. "It's just part of intel," he says with a shrug, like creeping on people is some casual hobby. "But I know more than just what positions you like. I know you're pregnant."

My blood turns to ice.

Jack's grin widens, relishing my horror. "See, there *is* a little more to this than just money. Nico and his old man? They pushed the families to move away from the *real* business— human trafficking, drugs, all the good stuff. That fucked me over. I lost money. Lots of it." He pauses. "So yeah, I want revenge. And what better way to get it than taking out the mother of Nico's unborn kid? That'll hurt him in ways you can't even imagine."

I'm speechless. My stomach lurches. He knows I'm pregnant, and he's planning on using it to destroy Nico. Before I can respond, there's a knock at the door.

Jack barks, "Come in!" and the door swings open.

One of his goons steps in, looking smug. "Boss, you won't believe this—Nico Conti himself is here. Says he wants to come to an arrangement. Don't worry – he's alone, and we patted him down."

Jack bursts into laughter. "Oh, does he now? Send him in." He glances at me, his grin shifting into something darker. "But first, gag the girl."

The goon grabs a rag and binds my mouth before tying my arms to the chair. I try to wriggle free, but he yanks the ropes tight, pulling the chair to the corner. I glare at him, but it's no use.

Jack settles behind his desk, leaning back with a smug look on his face. Moments later, Nico walks through the door. My heart practically leaps out of my chest—*he's here.*

Relief floods through me, but so does fear. Jack's smug look tells me Nico is walking straight into danger.

Even through my panic, I can't help the way Nico's presence stirs something in me. The sight of him—so strong, so calm, despite everything—does things to me I wasn't prepared for.

Nico's eyes flicker toward me, and I can tell he's holding back his rage.

"I'm here to talk."

Jack smirks. "Then have a seat."

As Nico moves toward the desk, I notice something—the goon pulled my chair to a spot where I can see *behind* Jack's desk. Something there catches my eye. I squint, trying to figure out what I'm seeing. My heart skips a beat when I realize what it is—a gun. *Jack's planning to kill Nico right here.* Panic surges through me, but I can't just scream or thrash around. I've got to be smart.

Nico's eyes flick over to me, his expression calm, asking without words if I'm okay. I nod slowly, trying to keep my face neutral while my mind races for a way to warn him.

Jack leans back in his chair, his grin never faltering. "So, Conti, what exactly do you want?"

Nico's voice is cold but steady. "I want Willow. That's it. No more bloodshed."

As they talk, my mind scrambles for a plan. Then it hits me —I can chew through the gag. It'll take time, but if I start now and subtly, slowly chew, maybe I can get it off before it's too late. I bite down carefully, working the fabric between my teeth, slow enough not to attract attention.

Nico keeps his eyes on Jack. "I know you're the one who killed my father. But I'm willing to let that go, *if* you step back now. Let Willow go."

I chew faster, my heart racing. I have to get this gag off before Jack pulls that trigger.

Nico doesn't know how close he is to danger.

Jack laughs, leaning forward. "Well, alright, Conti. Let the negotiations begin."

CHAPTER 35

"I want Willow out of here. Unharmed."

My gaze is locked on Jack, every fiber of my body screaming to rip him apart, but I hold it in. I can't let rage take over—*not yet*.

Jack throws his head back and laughs like I've just told the funniest joke he's ever heard. "And give up my best bargaining chip? Not a chance, Conti."

I grit my teeth, my fists clenching. "You're screwed either way, Jack. Might as well make it less painful for yourself in the end."

Jack leans back in his chair, smirking. "Is this your idea of negotiation, Conti? You threaten me, and I... what, hand her over? Beg for my life?" He scoffs, shaking his head. "You've lost your edge."

The sight of Willow bound like that, gagged and terrified, makes the blood boil in my veins. Every second I stand here, looking at her like that, I want to put a bullet between Jack's eyes.

But I can't—not with his two goons lurking behind me, ready to pounce. Not to mention the little detail that I'm unarmed.

Jack knows it, too. He sees the rage in my eyes and takes his shot. "What's the matter, Nico? Can't protect your little toy? Should've stuck to being just her boss. You're in over your head, and now look at her. You know, I'm thinking of taking her for a spin after you're dead." He grins, his eyes flashing with sick enjoyment. "Bet she'd be real fun."

I swallow the fury rising in my throat. Jack's trying to bait me, but I won't let him win. I need to buy time. I clench my fists, trying to keep my voice steady. "What is it you want, Jack? What's your endgame?"

Jack leans back in his chair, acting like he's got all the time in the world. "What I want? I want this city back how it was before your old man fucked it up by playing Mr. Morality." He waves his hand in the air, like the thought disgusts him. "Ten years ago, I was making money hand over fist. Then your dear old dad came in and cut half my business."

I snort, shaking my head. "Maybe you shouldn't have been running in the human trafficking business."

Jack's eyes flash, but he keeps his grin. "I went where the money was, Conti. Always have, always will." He shrugs, brushing off the moral high ground like it's nothing. "But that's in the past. No matter. Things will go back to how they were."

My jaw clenches, but I can't let him see how close I am to breaking. I glance at Willow, hoping she's holding up. That's when I notice it—her mouth is moving under the gag. She's *chewing through it*. Smart girl.

I keep my eyes from lingering on her too long, not wanting to tip Jack off. The longer I keep this going, the more time Willow has. We're close. I just need to keep this bastard talking until the moment's right.

I keep my tone steady, eyes locked on Jack. "I showed up in good faith, ready to talk."

Jack throws his head back in laughter, the sound cold and sharp. "Good faith? Says the man who tried to torture me to death in his basement."

My eyes narrow. "You killed my father. You earned every second of that."

Jack's grin falters, replaced by something darker. He leans forward, his voice dripping with venom. "Let's cut the bull-shit, Conti. I brought you here to *suffer*. This ends one way —with a bullet in your head."

Before I can respond, the sound of gunshots echoes from downstairs. Jack's head whips toward the door, eyes wide with panic.

I can't stop the grin that spreads across my face. "I didn't come here to negotiate either, Jack. I came here to get you talking long enough for my boys to move in."

Realization dawns on Jack's face, his fury bubbling over. He stands up, knocking over his chair, rage flashing in his eyes. But it's too late. He knows exactly what's happening now, and it's out of his control.

The room erupts into chaos. Jack's goons are panicking, looking to him for orders. "What do we do, boss?" one of them yells, but Jack just growls, eyes locked on me.

More gunshots ring out from downstairs, and I recognize the sound—my guys are packing serious heat, and from the sound of it, they're winning.

Jack clenches his fists, rage rolling off him. "It ends now, Conti."

Before he can move, Willow finally spits out her gag, screaming, "He has a gun!"

Jack moves fast, pulling a pistol from under his desk. He levels it at me, but I'm quicker. I grab the chair I've been sitting on and slam it into the goon behind me, knocking the wind out of him and sending his gun to the floor, where it lands with a clatter.

Jack fires, but his aim's off—he hits the goon by mistake, the man crumpling to the floor. Then Jack's gaze snaps to Willow, fury burning in his eyes. He turns the gun on her, finger on the trigger.

I slam my fist into the gut of the other goon, grabbing his gun before he can react. Just as I lift the weapon, I see Willow in the corner, frantically scooting her chair to the side. She topples over, her head slamming against the floor. My heart seizes as she goes limp, knocked unconscious.

Jack sees it too. He turns his gun on her, his finger tightening on the trigger. I don't hesitate. I raise the gun and fire.

The bullet hits Jack square between the eyes. His body jerks once before crumpling to the floor, dead before he hits the ground. The room falls silent, save for the thud of his lifeless body.

The door bursts open, Sal and the boys storming in, guns raised, ready to finish the job. They take in the scene—Jack's dead, and through the now-open door I can see his remaining men surrendering with their hands up, the fight completely drained out of them.

I rush over to Willow, my hands shaking as I undo her bindings. Her face is pale, her breathing shallow, and the sight of her like this makes me want to tear the whole world apart.

I gently cradle her in my arms, turning to my men.

"Hospital. Now."

CHAPTER 36

Everything's a blur as I slowly come to. My head is pounding like someone's banging a drum inside my skull. Then, the memories hit me all at once—Jack, the gun, the kidnapping.

Panic flares in my chest, but when I open my eyes, I don't see that grimy, shitty office. Instead, I'm in a calm, well-lit hospital room.

"Thank God—you're up," a familiar voice cuts through the haze.

I blink, my vision slowly clearing, and there he is. Nico. Relief washes over me as I see him approach, his expression a mix of worry and relief.

"Is this a dream?"

He gives me a soft smile, reaching out to brush a strand of hair off my forehead. "No, Willow. It's real. You're safe."

I stare at him, trying to process everything. Nico saved me. I'm alive. It feels too good to be true.

I try to piece together what happened, but it's all fuzzy. My thoughts feel jumbled, and I instinctively glance down at my body, checking for any signs of gunshot wounds or injuries.

Nothing. No blood, no bandages.

But then, it hits me.

"Oh my God... the baby," I mutter aloud, my hand flying to cover my mouth as the realization spills out. I just dropped the bomb on Nico. I glance at him, expecting shock, maybe even anger.

But he doesn't look surprised. In fact, he just smiles, his eyes softening. "The baby's fine," he says calmly.

Before I can even process how he knows, a couple of nurses rush in to check me over, asking the usual questions. *Are you in pain? How's your head?*

I answer them, but my mind's somewhere else. All I want is to talk to Nico, to find out how he knew about the baby and what really went down with Jack. Despite the chaos around me, the look on his face—so calm and warm—makes me feel like everything's going to be okay.

And for the first time in what feels like forever, I believe it.

One of the nurses smiles at me. "You've got a minor concussion from the fall, but nothing serious."

Before I can respond, Nico jumps in with, "Yeah, you need to be more careful when hanging pictures."

I blink, confused as hell for a second before I realize what he's doing. "Yeah, definitely should've used a step ladder instead of balancing on the end table. Stupid me, huh?"

"We'll hire a decorator for the nursery, no need to do everything yourself," Nice says, stunning me into silence.

The nurse smiles at us and tells me to press my call button if I need anything before leaving us alone.

"What happened?" I ask, cutting straight to it. "To Jack? His guys?"

Nico glances away for a second, like he's debating how much to unload on me. Typical. "Jack's been taken care of," he finally says, voice calm but loaded with layers. "There's not gonna be a war. Everything's good."

Nico's eyes meet mine again, searching for some kind of reaction. But I don't flinch. Instead, I give a small nod, letting him know I'm cool with whatever went down. I trust him.

And right now, that's all I need.

I can feel the worry bubbling up, even though everything seems calm now. Nico notices immediately, because of course he does.

"What's wrong?" he asks, his brows pulling together.

"How did you find out about the baby?"

He chuckles. "I had one of my guys hack into the records system to get a peek at your test results. I saw the blood work that confirmed you were pregnant. I'm sorry for violating your privacy, but I was so damn scared."

"It's okay, I forgive you. I'm so sorry I didn't tell you sooner. I wanted to; I swear. But then everything got insane, and I was trying to find the right time, and—"

Before I can ramble myself into a full-blown apology spiral, Nico leans in and *bam*—his lips crash against mine. Mid-sentence, no warning, just pure, earth-shattering kiss. It's like my brain short-circuits; I practically melt into the bed, my body forgetting how to do anything but *feel* him.

When he finally pulls back, I'm breathless, staring up at him like he just solved world peace.

"It's alright," he says, his voice low and soothing. "I'm thrilled about the baby."

"Really?"

"Of course." His eyes are soft, and for a second, everything feels perfect.

But his expression shifts. His jaw tightens, and he has a dark look in his eyes that makes my stomach flip. "What's wrong?" I ask, instantly on edge.

He hesitates for a moment, then looks at me with a weight in his gaze. "Is there any way you can forgive me?"

Nico drops down to one knee, gently taking my hand like he's about to propose or confess something wild. My heart's racing, and then he starts talking.

"I've kept things from you, Willow. Big things. ," he says, eyes locked on mine. "From the beginning. I wasn't open with you about who I really am. About my lifestyle, my criminal background. I never told you the kind of danger you could be in with me."

I blink, the weight of his words sinking in. He's got that serious, brooding look that makes my heart skip, but I stay quiet. Let him get it all out.

"And more than that," he continues, voice thick with guilt, ". I let you get kidnapped. You could've been killed." I squeeze his hand, trying to keep him grounded, but he's on a roll now. "On top of everything," he says, almost spitting the words out, "I've been a coward."

I frown. "A coward? Nico, you're literally anything but a coward."

He shakes his head, looking down like he's ashamed. "No. I am. Because I was too scared to tell you how I really feel about you."

My heart stutters. Oh. *Oh.*

"I love you, Willow," Nico says, his voice firm, leaving no room for doubt. "I've known it for a while, and I'm a damn fool for not telling you sooner."

My heart's doing this crazy little flip, like it's about to launch out of my chest. He loves me. *He loves me.*

"I didn't plan on falling in love or having another child. But I'm damn sure of one thing—I'm ready to be the man you deserve. If you can forgive me."

And then he just waits, looking up at me like he's expecting his whole world to come crashing down, like I'm the only person who could break him. I realize that I may be the only person in this city who's ever seen Nico look this vulnerable, this has me worried about what's coming next.

I put him out of his misery and tell him, "I love you too!" I'm practically vibrating with excitement.

The relief on his face is instant, and I swear, it's like a weight has been lifted off both of us. He pulls me into his arms, and in this moment, everything—*all* the chaos, all the danger—fades away. It's just us.

I gasp, my hands jumping to my mouth. "Oh my God, the girls. Are they okay?

Nico nods, his expression softening. "Your cousin and the twins made it home fine. Don't worry. Jack was smart enough not to mess with them—he knew better. He wouldn't have gotten off with just a quick end if he had."

I raise an eyebrow at the casual way he mentions Jack's "quick end" but decide not to dig. Probably better I don't know the details.

Nico leans back, a smirk playing on his lips. "The twins have been waiting to hear about you. They're eager to start Christmas shopping."

I can't help but laugh, imagining those two ready to tear through a mall. "Well, I'm going to need to get out of this hospital bed if we're going to start Christmas shopping."

He takes my hand again, his thumb brushing softly over my knuckles. "I can't wait to make you a part of my life. For real this time."

My heart swells. This man, this life—it's everything I didn't know I wanted. I lean in, and we kiss, soft and slow, like a promise.

Pulling back, I grin. "We can start by making this the best Christmas ever."

Nico smiles, eyes full of warmth.

"Deal."

Four days later, Christmas Eve...

We're rushing through the shops at Columbus Circle, the girls buzzing with excitement like they've downed five candy canes each. It's Christmas Eve, and Lucia and Giulia *insisted* on one last shopping trip before dinner.

Four years old, and they're already calling the shots.

Ms. M is trailing behind, trying to keep up with their energy. The woman's got fire in her, but even she's struggling to corral them in this crowd. Meanwhile, Willow's beside me, looking ready to chase them herself.

"Willow," I say firmly, cutting her off before she can even think about running after the twins. "Relax. You're pregnant, remember? No chasing after those two."

She shoots me a sassy look, but I hold my ground. "I'm pregnant, not fragile."

I step in front of her again, my hand gentle but firm on her arm. "You're not fragile, but you *are* carrying our child. Let Ms. M handle it."

Lucia and Giulia dart ahead, laughing as they spot a toy store, completely unaware of the chaos they're causing. Ms. M throws me an exasperated look over her shoulder. I give her a nod. She's got this.

Willow huffs but relents, leaning into me with a small smile. "Fine, but next time, I'm not sitting on the sidelines."

I smirk. "We'll see about that."

We're walking together, side by side, keeping an eye on the twins. The girls are in their own world, but my attention is on Willow. I glance down at her, watching for any signs that she's pushing herself too hard.

"How are you feeling?"

"Fine," she says, giving me a small smile. "The concussion is pretty much gone."

"That's not what I meant," I say, stopping her with a look. "Not just the physical matters. What you've been through—it doesn't disappear just because you can't see the wounds."

She pauses for a second, leaning into me. "It was scary. I'm still a little shaken up, I won't lie. But it's over now. Jack's gone. And more importantly, I know you're watching out for me."

I wrap an arm around her waist, pulling her closer. "Always," I tell her, my voice low but full of promise. "I'll *always* watch out for you."

She tilts her head up, meeting my eyes. I see the trust in their depths. No matter what's happened, she knows I've got her back. That's all that matters.

The girls' laughter echoes around us, pulling me back to reality.

We stop in front of the toy shop, watching through the glass as Lucia and Giulia dart around, eyes lit up, already hunting for the perfect gifts for each other. I keep one eye on them, but my focus shifts to Willow.

"Are you looking forward to tonight?" I ask.

She looks up at me with that smile—the one that always knocks me off balance. "Yeah, I am. My first Christmas Eve with the girls and you as... whatever it is we are now."

I chuckle. "Yeah, we haven't exactly figured that part out yet, have we?"

She grins, her eyes playful. "Nope. I guess we skipped the whole formal exit interview for my nanny services."

I give the matter a moment of thought. "Alright, how about this? Ms. M takes over with the girls for the next week or two. I'll bring in extra help for the house. Consider the next couple of weeks your Christmas break—time to process everything."

I watch as relief washes over her, softening her expression. "I'd like that," she says, leaning in a little closer. I tighten my grip on her hand.

The girls come bursting out of the shop, each of them clutching something behind their backs, barely able to contain their excitement.

"Papa, Willow! We got each other presents!" Giulia announces. , eyes wide with pride.

Lucia bounces on her toes, holding hers tightly. "But we can't show each other yet! Can you hide them, Willow?"

Willow smiles, crouching down to their level. "Of course. I'll keep them safe."

Both girls eagerly hand over their carefully chosen gifts, trusting her without hesitation. She tucks them into her purse with a smile, and I watch the way she fits into this moment so naturally. It's like she's always been here, a part of this family.

"Alright, girls," I say, drawing their attention. "Ready to head home for Christmas Eve dinner?"

They both nod, eyes gleaming with excitement as they race toward the car. We all pile in, the driver pulling away, the city lights flashing past as the girls chatter nonstop about tomorrow—what Santa might bring, what they want to do first thing in the morning. Ms. M chimes in, trying to keep them from getting too hyper, but I can see she's losing that battle.

As I listen to their voices, my phone buzzes. I glance down at the screen.

Sal: *The Rossis are keen to meet after Christmas. They're ready to discuss terms for a formal peace treaty.*

I read it over twice, a sense of satisfaction settling in. We'd been on the brink of war not long ago, but now we're about to seal the deal and make sure it doesn't happen.

We pull up to the townhouse, and the place is lit up like a damn Christmas card. The lights, the wreaths, the trees—it's all decked out, festive as hell. I can't help but smile. This is what Willow's brought to my life—warmth, life, a real home. She's made this place feel like more than just walls and security.

The girls pile out, racing inside, and we follow. The chef is in the kitchen, putting the finishing touches on the Christmas feast. Roasted prime rib, garlic mashed potatoes, roasted Brussels sprouts, and a pear and walnut salad. Dessert? A classic—chocolate Yule log with whipped cream.

The girls and Ms. M head into the den to finish wrapping the last of the presents. I watch them go, but Willow hangs back, lingering near me with a mischievous look in her eyes.

"I've been meaning to check out what you've been doing with the gym downstairs," she says, her voice low and teasing.

I grin, stepping closer, lowering my voice to match hers. "You can unwrap that present in the morning."

She winks, not missing a beat. "I've got something in mind you can unwrap *tonight*."

I smirk, reaching out to give her a playful squeeze on her ass. She gasps, but I can tell by the way her lips curl into a smile that she loves it.

"Careful," I murmur, leaning in close. "Or I'll unwrap it right now."

Her laughter fills the air, and damn if it doesn't make me want her even more.

Dinner's perfect. Once we're done, the girls rush into the den, begging to watch a Christmas movie.

We settle on *Home Alone*—classic enough to keep everyone entertained, including Ms. M, who's already into it.

The girls do their best to stay awake, determined to catch Santa in the act, but it's no use. Within minutes after the movie's over, they're curled up in front of the fire, out cold, their tiny snores mixing with the crackling flames.

I scoop up both Lucia and Giulia, one in each arm, carrying them up to their room. Willow's right there beside me, helping me tuck them in under their cozy blankets. The warmth of the moment settles between us as we watch them sleep, their little faces peaceful.

"They're perfect," Willow whispers, leaning into me. "I'm so happy they're in my life."

I don't say it, but the thought hits me hard. She's the right woman to be their new mother, to stand by my side.

As we quietly leave the room, Ms. M catches us at the door. She gives us a knowing look, waving her hand. "Go on, you two. I'll take the monitor and stay in the guest room tonight."

"Thank you, Olivia."

We make our way back down to the den, where the fire's still burning low, casting the room in a warm glow.

Willow grins, her eyes gleaming with mischief. "Time for a little holiday cheer."

In a heartbeat, I pull her close, pressing my lips to hers. The kiss is deep, intense, like we're making up for all the moments we've held back. Her hands are in my hair, and I've got my arms wrapped around her, pulling her tight against me.

I pause, just for a second, breaking the kiss. "I love you," I say, my voice low, serious. "And I'll do anything for you."

Her face softens, and I catch the glisten of tears in her eyes. She smiles, the kind of smile that tells me she feels it just as much as I do. "I love you too," she whispers, before pulling me back in.

Before long, we're on the floor in front of the fire, our hands working quickly to slip each other out of our clothes. The heat between us has nothing to do with the flames burning nearby—it's all us, wrapped up in each other, lost in the moment.

I strip her bare, taking my time, and when I finally sit up to take her in, I can't help but grin. Her skin practically glows, that subtle shift happening already, even though she's only six weeks pregnant. It's like she's got this new light about her, and I feel this surge of pride knowing she's carrying our future inside her.

"You're staring," she says, a teasing smile on her lips.

"Can you blame me? Look at you," I murmur, running my hand over the curve of her hips. "You're even sexier now carrying my kid."

She bites her lip, giving me a mischievous look. "Oh, yeah?"

I laugh, leaning down to kiss her neck. "Yeah. You're already glowing, baby."

Her smile softens, and I can feel the love in the way she looks up at me. There's hunger there, too—she wants me just as much as I want her.

I move between her legs, teasing her, letting my cock rest right at her entrance. She gasps a little, her hands immediately sliding down to grab my ass, pulling me closer.

"Stop teasing," she breathes, her voice almost a plea.

I chuckle, pressing just a little deeper. "Say please."

"Please."

That's all it takes. I push inside, slow and steady, and the warmth of her wraps around me, pulling me deeper. Every inch feels incredible, like I'm right where I'm supposed to be.

"God, I love you," I groan, feeling her tighten around me.

She pulls me closer, her breath hot against my skin. "Show me."

I thrust into her slowly at first, savoring the way she feels—tight, hot, wrapped around me like she was made for this. Every time I move, she gasps, her back arching beneath me, and I can't take my eyes off her. She looks incredible, her skin flushed, breasts bouncing with each thrust, and those eyes of hers—half-lidded, staring up at me with pure desire.

"You like that?" I ask, my voice low and rough.

Her lips part, a soft moan escaping as she digs her nails into my back. "Yes... God, yes."

I smirk, leaning down to kiss her neck, picking up the pace, the sound of our bodies coming together filling the room.

Each time I push deeper, her breath hitches, her legs wrapping tighter around my waist.

"Faster," she whispers, her voice shaky with need.

I give her exactly what she's begging for, slamming into her harder, faster, feeling her body start to tremble underneath me. She's close, I can feel it—her breathing is ragged, her grip on me tightening.

"You're going to come for me, aren't you?" I growl in her ear.

She nods, barely able to speak through the pleasure. "I'm— so close."

I push deeper, thrusting faster, watching her body tense up, her face twisting with pleasure. "Come for me," I command, my voice firm.

And she does. Her whole body shudders, back arching off the floor, her lips parting in a breathless cry as she falls apart beneath me, clenching tight around me.

I hold back my own release, watching her unravel.

She grins at me, a playful glint in her eyes, then her hands are on my legs, pushing me back. I let her guide me, enjoying the shift in control. She climbs over me, her body glistening, and I can't help but smirk.

"I love it when you get bossy like this," I say.

She leans down, her lips brushing against mine. "I know," she whispers.

."

Her hands slide down to my cock, fingers wrapping around it, and I groan at the feel of her grip. She lines me up, holding it steady, and slowly starts to lower herself.

I watch, my breath catching as she takes me in, inch by inch. She's so slick, so wet, that I slide inside her perfectly, her body stretching to fit me.

It's intoxicating, watching her move like this—her hips sinking, breasts bouncing slightly, her lips parting as she takes me deeper. She's in complete control, and it's driving me wild.

"Fuck, you feel incredible," I growl, gripping her hips., watching her face as her pussy swallows me whole.

Her breath hitches, and her eyes close for a second as she settles, fully seated on my cock. The heat of her, the tight, wet pressure—it's overwhelming.

She's got me exactly where she wants me, and the way she rolls her hips, slow and deliberate, makes it clear she knows exactly what she's doing.

And all I want is more.

EPILOGUE II

WILLOW

I'm on top of him, loving every second of it.

The view? God, it's perfect—his chest rising and falling under me, muscles flexing as he grips my hips, eyes dark with lust, watching every move I make. The fire's roaring behind us, casting a warm glow across his skin, and it feels like it's fueling the heat between my thighs.

The way he fills me, how perfectly he fits, it's almost too much... but in the best way possible.

I start bucking my hips harder, riding him like I own him, and the groan rumbling out of his chest makes me smile. He leans up, his mouth finding my nipples, sucking, teasing, sending jolts of pleasure straight through me.

His hands slide from my hips to my ass, squeezing hard, guiding me to move exactly how he wants it.

"You like this?" I pant, breathless but still cocky.

He looks up at me, gray eyes burning with desire. "Love it. Keep going, baby."

I grin, rolling my hips in slow circles just to tease him, knowing exactly what it does. "You're so easy."

He laughs, a low, rough sound that sends a shiver down my spine. "For you? Always."

His hands tighten on my ass, pulling me down hard, and I let out a gasp, loving how deep he is. I lean down, my lips brushing his ear. "You going to come for me, or do I need to work you a little harder?"

That smirk of his? Dangerous as ever. "Give it your best shot."

He sits up suddenly, pulling me in tight by the waist, and I let out a loud gasp as I grind down harder onto him. I'm riding him like crazy, feeling his thick cock stretch me in all the right ways, every thrust sending shockwaves through me.

My whole body's on fire, and I'm not even trying to hold back—I'm screaming his name, and his deep groans tell me he's just as close.

"Baby, I'm gonna come," he growls, voice strained.."

"Same," I pant, barely able to get the words out.."

I slam down one more time. My body shudders as I come hard, my walls tightening around him, and he follows, erupting inside me. I can feel the heat of his release flooding into me, and it's so intense, so raw, I swear I see stars for a second. We're clinging to each other, lost in the moment, bodies trembling together as we ride out the high.

When we finally crash to the ground, we're both panting, still wrapped up in each other. He pulls me close, his lips finding mine in a soft, lingering kiss.

"I love you," I whisper against his lips.

"I love you too," he murmurs, his hands stroking my hair. "I'll watch over you forever, Willow. You and the girls and the baby."

I laugh softly, looking up at him, still catching my breath. He brushes a strand of hair from my face, his touch tender despite the wild ride we just had.

"Best Christmas ever?" he asks, a grin spreading across his face, that cocky smirk I can't get enough of.

I bite my lip, pretending to think about it, but I can't hold back my smile. "So far? Hell yes."

I wake up next to Nico, the warmth of his body still pressed against mine. We'd slipped upstairs to continue our love-making in bed before falling into a deep slumber.

Before I can even fully shake off sleep, the door bursts open, and the girls come rushing in, bouncing on the bed. I sit up, groaning.

"Merry Christmas!" they squeal, practically vibrating with excitement.

Ms. M follows behind them, her hands up in surrender. "I tried to hold them off as long as I could, but... it *is* Christmas."

I laugh, giving the girls hugs and kisses, Nico doing the same. "Okay, okay, we're up!"

We shuffle downstairs, and the girls immediately dive into their presents, paper flying everywhere. It's chaos, the kind you love on a morning like this.

Nico walks over to Ms. M, who's watching with a smile from the kitchen. He hands her a small box, and she looks surprised. "For you," he says with a grin. "From Willow and me."

She opens it to find a beautiful silver bracelet with tiny charms—each one representing a memory or a place she's mentioned from home in Italy. Her eyes well up a little, and she gives Nico a tight hug. "*Grazie mille*, you both, it's beautiful."

I nudge Nico, handing him my gift. He unwraps it to reveal a gorgeous pair of house slippers. "A little hint to take it easy every now and then," I joke.

He laughs, pulling me in for a kiss. "I love it. But your present's downstairs."

He grins, and my curiosity spikes.

The girls are practically bouncing in place, barely able to contain their excitement. "You're gonna love it! We helped!" they chirp in unison.

I laugh, already intrigued. "Okay, okay, let's see this masterpiece."

We all rush downstairs, heading straight for Nico's home gym, and the second I step inside, my jaw drops. Part of his gym has been completely transformed—not just into a yoga corner, but a full-on video studio for my YouTube lessons.

"Oh my God, Nico!" I gasp, eyes wide.

He grins, clearly pleased with himself. "I know you've been wanting to take your yoga classes to the next level, so I thought why not? It's got everything you need—studio lighting, a camera setup that's already hooked up to the stream, soundproofing so no interruptions, and a bunch of backdrops depending on your mood for the day."

I walk further in, my heart pounding with excitement as I take it all in. Then the girls tug on my sleeve, pointing to the wall. "Look!" they say, giggling. I spot their tiny handprints in colorful paint on the corner of the studio wall, and next to them, a set of new yoga mats they picked out. One's got stars, the other, unicorns.

Tears prick my eyes as I turn to Nico. "You did all this for me?"

He nods, his smile softening. "It's a stepping stone to your own business, for whenever you're ready."

I throw my arms around him, then scoop the girls into the hug too. "I love you all so much. This is... perfect."

"I love you too," Nico murmurs, kissing the top of my head.

Best. Christmas. Ever.

~

One year later...

I'm in the middle of a lesson, and even a year later I still can't believe how perfect this setup is. The massive TV on the wall shows a grid full of tiny windows—at least a hundred people tuning in from all over the world, no more squinting at my tiny MacBook mid-stretch. Now I'm actually teaching, not juggling tech.

"Alright, everyone, let's move into our final pose—child's pose," I say, settling back on my heels and extending my arms forward, feeling the stretch down my spine. "Take a deep breath in, and exhale slowly... let your body relax."

I scan the screen, watching people from every time zone melt into the pose. It's surreal, seeing my little yoga community grow like this. I guide them through a few more breaths, my voice calm and steady, even though I'm buzzing with excitement inside.

Right on cue, I hear the baby monitor crackle to life, followed by a tiny, insistent wail. I can't help but laugh.

"Well, looks like my little man knows when it's time to wrap up," I tell the class with a grin. "Thanks for joining me today, everyone. Same time next week!"

I wave goodbye and shut off the feed, smiling as I head upstairs to check on the baby. As I walk, I can't help but think about how far things have come. My classes are taking off, I'm reaching more people than I ever imagined, and best of all? I'm having a blast doing it.

Life is good.

It's the Christmas season again, and the whole house feels alive with a festive buzz. I head upstairs to the kitchen, where Lucia and Giulia are sitting at the table, happily munching on pancakes while Ms. M handles the morning routine until the new nanny arrives.

"Morning, girls," I say, ruffling their hair as I pass by.

Lucia looks up with a grin. "How was yoga, Mommy?"

Mommy. I didn't even ask them to start calling me that – they did it all on their own.

"It was great! We had people from *all* over the world today," I say, grabbing a quick sip of coffee.

"Can we see the baby?" Giulia pipes up, her little voice full of excitement.

I smile at her. "I'm going to feed him first, then you can cuddle him, okay?"

Giulia nods, satisfied. "Can we start decorating for Christmas after?"

"Oh, for sure. Let's deck this place out," I reply with a wink.

I head upstairs, coffee in hand, feeling that familiar warmth of holiday cheer as I peek into the nursery. And there he is —Nico, already up with our baby boy, Luca. He's cradling him in his strong arms, softly bouncing and humming, while Luca's little fingers clutch at his shirt.

I stop in the doorway, my heart swelling. It never gets old seeing Nico—this big, strong man—being so tender with our son. The contrast is always a little mind-blowing. For someone who's all muscle and testosterone, he's an absolute softie when it comes to Luca.

I stand in the doorway for a moment, just watching them, feeling like the luckiest person in the world.

As I watch Nico with Luca, my mind drifts to the life he's tied to—the mob life he works so hard to keep me and the kids out of. The last time we really talked about it was a little less than a year ago, right after the treaty between the families was signed.

He'd said there should be peace for a while, and he'd seemed so sure. But I know better. There's always a darker side, always something lurking beneath the surface. That world never really goes away, but I have to admit—he's made good on his promise to keep us safe.

I walk over to him, wrapping my arms around his waist and kissing his cheek. He smiles, that soft look he always gets when he's with Luca.

"Morning, Mama," he says, his voice low and warm.

I look down at our baby boy with my nose and Nico's intense gray eyes. He's already such a heartbreaker.

"He's too handsome for his own good."

Nico chuckles, his thumb brushing over Luca's cheek. "Takes after his old man."

I roll my eyes, smirking. "And a bit of his mom, thank you very much."

Nico grins, his eyes softening as he looks at me. "Yeah, definitely got the best of both of us."

I smile, feeling the familiar warmth bloom in my chest as I take our son from him and cuddle him close.

Nico walks over to the window and pushes it open. The crisp air sweeps in, and I'm hit with the sight of a perfect, snowy day outside—everything is blanketed in fresh, untouched white. It's like something out of a postcard, so perfectly Christmas-y I almost laugh. But then, I catch the strange look on Nico's face.

"What is it?" I ask, narrowing my eyes.

He sighs, turning to me with a serious expression that always makes my stomach flip. "There's something I need to ask you."

My heart skips a beat, and a wave of worry washes over me. "Nico, what's going on?"

He shakes his head quickly. "No, nothing bad, I promise. I wanted to wait until Christmas, but... I just can't wait anymore."

Before I can say anything, he reaches into the pocket of his suit jacket and pulls out a small box. My breath catches, and I gasp, eyes widening when I realize what's happening. *No way*.

Nico looks at me with those stormy gray eyes, his voice soft but steady. "Willow, you've brought more joy to my life than I ever thought possible. You've made this house a home, not just for me, but for the girls too. You've completed our little family."

He opens the box, and there it is—a ring. My heart just about bursts.

"Willow," he says, his voice thick with emotion. "Will you marry me?"

Tears fill my eyes as I look at him, then down at Luca, then back at him. "Yes," I whisper, barely able to get the word out. "Yes, of course."

He pulls me in, kissing me deeply, and it feels like our own little happily ever after.

The End

If you loved Willow and Nico's story, then you will love more bestsellers from my Silver Fox Daddies series, including Sexting the Silverfox, an Amazon Top 23 bestseller.

Here's what readers had to say about Sexting the Silverfox:

★★★★★ "Be prepared. This couple is very hot together...I've read a lot of romance in my reading career. The author delivered a very well written story. I had to finish this one in a single day. It was imperative to find out how everything turned out." - Laura W., Goodreads Review

★★★★★ "Phenomenally written, with an outstanding storyline." -Heather D., Goodreads Review

★★★★★"Their chemistry was undeniable." -Knight L., Goodreads Review

★★★★★ "Hold on tight for a roller coaster ride!!!! Well worth reading!!!" -Tammy N., Goodreads Review

Made in the USA
Monee, IL
17 November 2024

70354081R00164